A N

A

Mystery

M. Culler

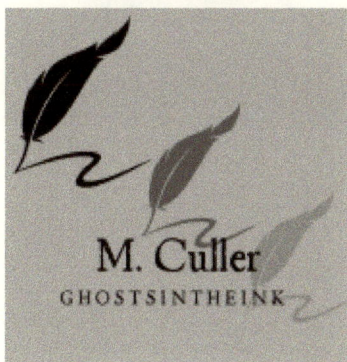

M. Culler

GHOSTSINTHEINK

Copyright Information

electronic, without the author's express permission and consent.

Cover Art: All images are free for use and in the public domain. Cover Design by V. McKevitt.

Dedications

To Phil, Morgana, and Malcolm- You love me, cheer me on, and put up with me. I love you so much.

To my parents, who encourage me, from scribbles to publication.

To Grandma Gladys. I know you're smiling. I wish I could see it.

To Tabby, Twinkle, Rosamunde, Ein, Brahms, and Rascal- the cats and dogs who leave pawprints on my heart.

To Annee Jones, who organized this whole shebang.

To the students who come to Mrs. Culler's Writing Club. You make writing cool.

To Judy, my darling editor.

To Rachelle, Jen, Laura, Sara, Shannon, Evan, Hebi, Kathleen, Katherine, Steve, Kathryn, Lauriel, Terry, Sofia, Michelle, Dawn, and Lolo—you talk me off of ledges that I build all by myself.

To The Mid-Atlantic Authors' Society and David Stockar, my partner in crime.

To Harry, the memoirist, book maven, one-man PR firm, and mobile therapist. You are valued and loved.

Soli Deo Gloria.

Introduction
New Year's Cataclysm

Davida Maxwell has one night to make sure her entire year goes right. As the new owner of the New Hope Animal Shelter, all she needs is one blockbuster gala, complete with donors with deep pockets, to turn a dilapidated building into a dream come true.

New Year's Eve could set her up for a bright future.

Or it could ruin her career and her reputation.

When the gala's biggest donation goes missing, Davida knows that she will be viewed as incompetent at best, or a thief at worst.

With midnight looming, go-getter Davida has three goals:

Distract the guests.

Keep Sparkler, the shelter's kitten mascot, out of the punch bowl.

Solve the mystery and find the missing money!

Can she do it all by New Year's Day? Or is this New Year's Eve just the start of a new disaster?

A New Year's Cat-aclysm by M. Culler is a cozy mystery with a twist of holiday romance that you're sure to love! Check out the other books in the Holiday Pet Sleuths series!

CHAPTER ONE

"I think you should have named him Houdini."

Davida laughed as she took the black and white handful from Nikki's outstretched arms. "When I got him, I didn't know that he would be able to get out of any cat carrier ever made." Davida raised the kitten above her head and looked into the adorable elfin face with its petite features and patches of black on fluffy white fur. "No prison can hold you, huh, Sparkler?"

In response, the kitten waved his tail. Sparkler's tail was long, skinny, and coal black from the rump until the very tip, where it seemed to explode in a riot of white puffy fur. When Davida had taken in the small survivor of an unwanted litter, he had been prowling around inside a big cardboard box, his tail held up over the side like a sparkler held in a child's hands.

"Maybe he needs some other kittens to play with?" Nikki suggested.

"Yeah, that would help." Davida nodded, but then shrugged. Right now, Sparkler was the only kitten resident. The end of December was not a popular time for new kittens. "If he had been born just a few weeks earlier, he would have probably been somebody's Christmas gift."

"Yeah," Nikki said with a frown, "and back here by Valentine's Day."

Sadly, it was true. Shelters always surged with returned Christmas puppies and kittens just a few months after the holiday. Little was cute, but babies grew. The bigger the animal, the faster the novelty wore off. It was no surprise that most of the dogs currently living at Davida's fledgling New Hope No-Kill Shelter were over a year old and mostly larger breeds. A handful were younger, summer puppies bought as end-of-school presents. Now that the kids were back at school, parents were stressing over another creature to care for and kids weren't living up to their promises to walk and feed Fido. Puppies from well-off families who'd chewed up Louboutins or left piddle puddles on the carpet were packed off to trainers, dog walkers, and doggy daycare, but not everyone had those resources. The unfortunate ones ended up in shelters, blamed for normal dog behaviors when neglectful humans were really the culprits.

The original New Hope No-Kill Shelter had opened in New Jersey as one of the first no-kill shelters in the country. They had started with one branch and a bunch of foster homes. Davida couldn't wait to open the first New Hope shelter in Maine—provided she actually had the space to keep it running. Right now, the old Pembroke Manor was more historical eyesore than functional.

But after Friday night, that was all going to change.

"Nikki, are you bringing a date on Friday night? If you are, did you make him RSVP and buy a ticket, or are we comping him?" Davida asked, checking her email. Another dozen RSVPs. She forgot to pause long enough for Nikki to answer.

"Yes! Officially over two hundred and fifty on the guest list. Maybe one more social media push will get us to three hundred, and that'll be capacity. After we finish renovating the place, the ground floor can probably hold five hundred. Right?"

"Uh... I don't know. Maybe ask the fire marshal? Or the health inspector? Look, about Friday night—" Nikki twisted her long, beaded braids nervously.

Davida was too excited to give her only full-time paid assistant the attention she deserved. She put the last RSVPs in the spreadsheet and sighed. "Okay, we have ten thousand. If we get another ten thousand in donations— and at least two local politicians said they're bringing big money and they want pictures taken with the press. Jenny Wheatly from *The Express* says she's coming for a few hours, but she's going to cover some other events, too. I'm thinking we'll have a photo op spot by the French windows, and we'll tell everyone who donates more than the hundred-dollar ticket cost that their pictures will go on the Wall of Wags."

"What the heck is the Wall of Wags? *Where* is it?" Nikki demanded.

"Well, we don't have it yet, but we will. It'll be a wall in the office with all the donor pictures. Is that tacky? I don't care." Davida marched away from her laptop and stared out the window at the sprawling two-story period home across the lawn. Right now, the old detached garage (which was double the size of Davida's first apartment) was serving as the shelter's office and canine kennel.

"Well, they're the ones who wanted pictures taken," Nikki pointed out, carrying a case of canned cat food to the back partition.

"I know, and I don't begrudge them the fame for doing a good deed. If I were rich, you *know* I'd be putting all my money into this adventure."

Nikki laughed, "You're poor and you are already putting all of your money into this adventure!"

"Hey, hey, that's not *exactly* right. I wasn't poor *until* I started chasing this dream. You know how it is. People fall in love with a dream and they do crazy things to make it happen."

"Well, not too crazy, I hope." Nikki gave her a strange look.

Davida waved the look away with a shrug. "Don't worry. I'm not going to do anything reckless. I mean, there's not much more I could do. I've already sunk everything I earned at my last job into the down payment on this place. The gala has to hit at least thirty-thousand for us to get the full matching grant from the New Hope Foundation to cover the first year's operating costs. Under the contract, we are responsible for half of the vet's salary, with the other half coming from private pay patients." Davida ran over figures in her head, bottom lip indented by her upper teeth as she calculated her gamble for the hundredth time that day, the millionth time this year.

"I got it, honey. The initial grant and your savings got us off the ground, but the gala needs to make us fly." Nikki pursed her lips, her large brown eyes following Davida as she scribbled another note on her ever-growing to-do list. "Don't worry, Davida. You'll make your money back in—"

"I'm not worried because I'll lose the money I put in." That wasn't exactly true. Davida skimmed over the yawning pit of anxiety that made the bottom drop out of her stomach whenever she thought about losing the start-up investment. "I'm worried because without a vet in attendance and the first year's funding, New Hope's records indicate most no-kill shelter models fail." Without that money to match their initial grants, the New Hope Foundation wouldn't allow their name to be on a shelter. They had hammered it home during Davida's training that when no-kill shelters fail, the dogs and cats they were saving ended up on the streets, in unsafe homes, or worse— shelters did not share the New Hope vision, "A new life and a new hope for all surrendered animals." "If we fail, we can't help anyone. The nearest shelter is in Portland, and they euthanize any unclaimed animal after thirty days. This has to work."

"It will. Stay positive. So, let's focus on what's going to go right. You've got your dress?"

Davida nodded, re-focusing, flexing her palms on her desktop in a centering gesture. "Just came last night and it fits."

"I'm sure your date will love you in it."

"Date? I'll be too busy hostessing. My only date is you." Davida looked at her right-hand woman with a smile. "I figured since both of us are single we might as well hit the gala together. We can stand around, look gorgeous, and snarf down cheese puffs when nobody's looking." Nikki bit her lip in a gesture that Davida had come to associate with guilt. "Nikki? Did you get a date? That's fine, I was only kidding about being single and snarfing. Well, about being single. I take my cheese puff sampling duties seriously." Davida's joke didn't alleviate the tension on Nikki's face. In fact, it spread to her own. "Nikki! You are absolutely coming to this event. You wouldn't leave me stranded by myself! I know I said I'd try to get a date, but I've just been so focused on the shelter that I haven't had time to meet anyone."

Nikki turned and started looking at the inventory lists. "Well, you'll have to take Sparkler. He's adorable and he's a cute mascot. I'll help you move one of those big three-tier cages over as soon as we're done."

Davida retrieved Sparkler from the top of a filing cabinet as he toppled into a half-open drawer. "You'll help me now but you're not showing up on Friday? This wasn't the plan! What's going on?"

Nikki stopped fighting her lip and tapping her short pink nails against the polished wood of the fourth-hand wooden wardrobe they used as a supply cabinet. "John Silversmith, a guy I used to date, is in town."

"So? Bring him with you! We'll let him come for free."

"He's in town, but not this one. He's about an hour away, but that's a lot closer than where he's been. We dated throughout college, but he transferred to a different branch after his college internship ended. John's been on the other side of the country for two years, which has meant he was out of my life... sort of. We stayed in touch. We haven't gotten serious about anyone else. We haven't dated anyone exclusively..."

"*He* says," Davida muttered, silently doubting every word.

"Look, he's with Whitehall and Kline Investments and he has a New Year's Eve mixer for a new branch that his company is opening in Portland. He asked me to go with him. Don't you see what this means? He wants to make this branch a success so that he can stay here and be closer. He wants to get back together!" Nikki rocked back and forth on her pink sneakers as if repressing the urge to jump up and down like a lovesick teen.

Davida put Sparkler in an empty laundry basket that was full of clean dog blankets and bedding. "Did he say all those things, Nikki?"

"No, but it's obvious," Nicki protested, pleading in her voice and eyes.

Davida said nothing. It was not obvious to her. Men were not to be trusted, and animals would always outweigh humans in her book. She felt a twinge of anger course through her as she realized that even Nicki was being decidedly "human" right now and abandoning the shelter for a shot at a guy who was probably just stringing her along.

Well, it's her life. She's young. You don't know what they had. Just don't say anything more. A smart person would keep her mouth shut, Davida thought.

I must not be that smart.

"Don't you think he's stringing you along? He has some event in the area and he knows you're around and available. You're a convenient date. You might be the 'other woman.' He could have a different woman at every branch, just like some sailors have girls in every port!"

Nikki crossed her arms. "Seriously?"

"No. Probably not. But can't you see him the next day? He won't be flying back the second the party ends, right? Don't do this, Nikki. The shelter needs you! The animals need you. You don't need a guy who suddenly pops up and wants you to make him look good but doesn't care about your plans."

"It's not like that. We've kept in touch and I know there's no one else. We still text every day. Look, this is a sign. He's my 'one.' Don't you believe in fate?"

"Nope." Davida knew she was being immature and short with her assistant. Her answer was terse.

"Okay, how about a little bit of New Year's magic?"

All of the sudden, Sparkler let out a yowl and streaked across the floor running headfirst into the wall on the trail of a tiny startled mouse.

Buy humane mouse traps. Davida scribbled another note on her list as she groaned, "No, I'm pretty sure I believe in a little New Year's catastrophe."

DAVIDA ADMITTED IT. She was sulking. She was twenty-nine and a full-grown woman (particularly full around the hips), and she knew better than to get angry at Nikki. It was just hard watching her associate and friend make the same mistakes Davida had made a few years before. After their awkward exchange, Nikki made herself scarce, leaving Davida and Sparkler alone in the office while she kept herself busy in the temporary kennel building. The kennel was partitioned off from the office but in the same former garage and workshop on the Pembroke Estate. Their small office/kennel was a red brick building up the winding drive from the main house.

"You know I don't want to get too attached to you," Davida told the pretty little kitten with its wide eyes and dandelion puff of a tail.

"Mew?" Sparkler looked at her entreatingly—and walked right off the edge of the card table that served as her desk, landing in the open tote bag by her feet.

"Well, if that isn't an omen," Davida muttered, retrieving the cat and settling it into her lap. Sparkler immediately curled into a tight ball, its poof of a tail tip between his front paws. The fluffy tuft of fur twitched and made the kitten sneeze as it dozed off.

"Hm. You're cute. Little. Unique. Freakishly adorable." Davida clicked off of her spreadsheets and opened a new window on her laptop. The New Hope Foundation had shelters all over the country, but hers was going to be the first in Maine. Each shelter owner went through rigorous requirements before being greenlighted by the foundation. Being part of the New Hope network was awesome, but each shelter had to manage their own operating costs through charitable donations, fundraising, and offering services that the community would pay for. In most cases, vets and groomers partnered with the shelter. Some offered boarding. Pembroke Manor would make the perfect shelter-slash-doggy daycare-slash-kennel.

Especially if social media worked its magic.

Davida unlocked her phone and opened her Vid-Up app, a social media video site. She aimed the camera at sleeping Sparkler and started recording. "Can you believe someone didn't want this absolutely adorable ball of fluff? Sparkler is sweet, affectionate, and the unofficial mascot for the Briarwood Branch of the New Hope Animal Shelter. Do you want to party with this silly baby boy? Check out our website to register for the New Year's Eve Gala. Dance the night away with a champagne buffet in a real 1920s estate. Put on your flapper dress, your dancing shoes, and practice your Charleston! Sparkler and I can't wait to see you at Paws and Prohibition at Pembroke!"

She hit the post button just as Sparkler stretched, yawned, and then sneezed as his own tail jabbed him in his tiny open mouth. With a startled "Mrowp!" the kitten rolled off her knees. Fortunately, Davida snagged him before he went into a free fall under the desk. "Dear Lord, cat. We're going to have to get you a crash helmet and body armor. I thought cats were supposed to be graceful."

Sparkler kneaded her leg as he settled back in her lap. The small white claws managed to prickle through her faded work jeans, a needle-like sensation making her wince. "Okay, okay. You didn't get the memo. That's okay. You have other things going for you." Davida smiled at her phone screen. The video already had a hundred hits. "You're a social media sensation, kitty."

Back to the spreadsheets.

Pembroke Manor was officially purchased, but still in need of renovations. The shelter needed equipment, both for the kennel areas and for the on-site vet's office. They needed the first year's salary for Nikki, the vet (who was supposed to start next week), and herself. Any extra could be used to fund part-time employees and start up a volunteer program.

She was pinning way too much on this New Year's Eve gala. What if it was a flop? At a hundred bucks a head and a three-hundred-person goal for the guest list, plus the additional donations... She tapped her calculator. Yes. That ought to get them to the threshold for New Hope to pick up the matching challenge while still covering the night's expenses. It helped that many of the locals were donating their time and talents.

Especially if Sparkler lured the people in.

Lost in worried thought, Davida jumped and almost sent Sparkler toppling from her lap when the phone rang. She grabbed the portable office phone and smiled, "New Hope Animal Shelter, Briarwood Branch. How can I help you?"

"Miss Maxwell. It's Preston Pembroke."

"Oh, Mr. Pembroke. How nice to hear from you." Davida's smile faded. It was not exactly a pleasure to hear from the middle-aged man, the son of the late Flora and Frederick Pembroke, one of the richest families in bustling little Briarwood, a coastal town in the southern region of Maine.

"Yes, fine, thank you."

She blinked at the phone. Had she asked how he was? From their previous encounters, she suspected Preston Pembroke was used to the sound of his own voice and the eager replies of the Yes Men he employed at his frozen food empire. "Uh. Thank you. How can I help you?"

"I've been thinking... I know you're setting up your little animal shelter—"

"New Hope is the largest no-kill shelter network in the country, Mr. Pembroke."

He continued as if she hadn't spoken, "But it's a shame to see that beautiful old house get turned into a giant piddle pad. My mother and father didn't fully appreciate the art deco style my grandparents envisioned when they had the place built in the 1920s."

"Ah." What else could she say? Flora and Frederick Pembroke hadn't lived in Pembroke Manor in the last twenty years, preferring their retirement condo in Florida. Mildred, known as Midge, the Pembroke's youngest daughter, had lived in a small downstairs section of the home, letting the rest slowly fall into disrepair. When Davida had first seen the property listed, she had actually believed it was a vacant, wooded lot. The sprawling two-story house with a broken-down tennis court, algae-choked pond, and weathered statuary had been completely invisible from the road.

"Midge shouldn't have sold it."

Tactfulness was not one of Davida's "spiritual gifts." "However, she did sell it. You signed off on it." Midge Pembroke had appeared at the broker's office, a tiny, gray-haired woman in a faded blue housecoat and slippers. It had shocked Davida to learn that the Pembroke's youngest child was only in her forties, but had always been a bit "simple." Mr. Pembroke and an agent from an assisted living facility had joined Midge at the office. Her brother had been impatient and blunt. The stranger from the nursing home had been gentle, explaining to Midge how she would have a safe, warm place with new friends and even a pet. But Pembroke Manor was too big for her to manage, and it wasn't safe to be alone.

"Anyone could see that Midge is deficient."

Davida bit her tongue. She'd been to see Midge several times since the timid woman had left the property and moved to Briarwood Court, an assisted living facility with bungalows surrounding a common dining and recreation area. Midge was lovely and sweet. The fact that she was also very childlike was no excuse to speak of her with disrespect. "I don't think deficient is the right word. Not at all. Your sister is beyond sufficient in warmth, love, kindness, decency—"

With an irritated huff, Pembroke cut Davida off. "Look, my parents left her the house so she'd have somewhere to live. They were right in thinking she'd never get married or hold down a job. Everyone in town knows they should have left it to me. Being a newcomer, you wouldn't know that."

Her tongue was going to be permanently scarred after this conversation. Yes, in Maine she would always be a newcomer since she hadn't been born there. But she had lived in Briarwood for almost a year, and most of that year had been very pleasant. The people in town loved their animals and looked forward to seeing something done with the decrepit old estate. Although it had become an eyesore, Pembroke Manor had once been famous for its lavish parties.

"Everyone in town seems to think that your parents did a good job dividing their assets among their kids. You got the bulk of the business. Midge got the house. Your brother got all of the vacation homes, the Florida retirement property, and rental properties. I may be a newcomer, but I pay attention."

Mr. Pembroke abruptly changed his tone and let out a hearty laugh. "You sure have got one ear to the ground. Well, I guess it'll come as no surprise to you to hear that I'm the brains of the family. Took my daddy's factory and turned it into a chain of factories in both Canada and the United States. With the supply chain issues we're facing overseas, manufacturing in the Lower Forty-Eight is a smart investment. Land in Portland is hellishly expensive, but Pembroke Manor isn't too far. If I clear cut all the woods, ripped up the lawns, and bulldozed the estate, I could have a new factory within driving distance from

Portland and a few hours from Boston. I'd like to buy the place back."

Davida dropped a heavy hand into her lap, startling the sleeping kitten. She spun in her chair, the motion of her body echoing her whirling mind.

But this place is perfect!

I don't want him to rip it up, even if he did live here as a kid! It's too beautiful.

Clearcut the woods? What will all the wild animals do?

Bulldoze the house? I've already got a dozen strays housed on site. I've hired a vet. I've hired Nikki. Heck, I've hired myself. This is my dream job and my dream. Period.

"I'm afraid I'm not interested."

"I'll pay you half-again Midge's selling price. The *original* selling price. $300,000."

"Oh."

Davida swallowed as the sound of imaginary rustling cash filled her ears. That was tempting. She'd been able to negotiate the purchase price of the property down to $180,000, so this offer was more than generous. But she'd already begun renovations, and she couldn't put a price on the blood, sweat, and tears she had invested. This property had so much potential, with space for the dogs to run, a place for the vet's office, a place to start boarding and training facilities, and more. She doubted she could find another property even half as suitable. If they kept the ballroom and kitchen intact after the big gala on New Year's Eve, they could even offer it up for events. Not many people would take advantage of it, but then again, she'd been to birthday parties at the SPCA as a kid and seen some famous people get married at zoos and museums. Why not have your special event at a beautiful animal shelter?

"Wh-what is it that you'd want to do with it again?" Davida stalled as she opened her operating costs and start-up costs spreadsheets. She scribbled figures on a pad as Pembroke lost his good-natured tones and repeated himself.

"I'm tearing down that old wreck of a place and putting up a factory, Miss Maxwell. It'll be good for the economy. Lots of jobs."

Her brow wrinkled at his last declaration. A lot of people in town had mentioned Preston Pembroke's factory, just outside of town, off of 295 North. Despite the local ties and the reasonable commute, only a few people in town worked there, claiming it didn't pay a living wage.

"I'm sure there would be plenty of jobs. But I'm not interested in selling at that price. I would need to scramble to find new premises and the approval period for a shelter to be approved by New Hope is usually around twelve months. I've already hired staff and started renovations. $400,000 would be the minimum I'd take." She crossed her fingers behind her back, as if the snarling man on the other end of the phone would be able to see her deception. In reality, she'd take less if she had to, but she *didn't* have to.

"That's hogwash. You're a greedy little—"

"I'm perfectly serious and not at all greedy. You're a businessman. I bought a property in need of massive renovations, and I've started them. To get approved for a new location with the minimum of required staff and equipment, I'd need to purchase a turn-key operation in a location zoned for animal facilities. That takes me right out of anything residential or highly industrial. Finding the perfect building in the perfect location will cost more. I'll need to recoup my outgo and pay off the contractors I've already hired. You know all this."

"But doubling your price is ridiculous. How much could you possibly spend on a bunch of animals?"

"You'd be surprised. Do we have a deal?" *Please say no.*

He said no, in a very colorful manner that forced her to hold the phone away from her ear.

"You took advantage of a senile old woman!"

"You were there! You told her to sign! Also, remember that when I showed up in that office to sign the paperwork, I'd never met you or your sister! I'd dealt with a realtor. Who got her that realtor? Who told her to accept my offer? Did you just want the money so that Briarwood Court would take her?" Davida demanded, rising and pacing with Sparkler under her arm.

Preston made a choking, snorting sound. "That's slander."

"Are you sure those weren't just *questions*? I asked if that's why you rushed through closing the deal for Pembroke Manor. Most private assisted living places expect you to pay up-front and out of pocket." Davida warmed to her topic. Sparkler, clearly enjoying a good performance when he saw one, dug his little claws in and made his way up to the collar of her worn pink overshirt, draping himself over one shoulder and headbutting her free ear.

"I... I..."

"You don't like when someone has no reason to say 'yes, sir, no, sir, how high, sir?' Do you? Well, I don't like being guilted at for wanting a fair deal. I went to see Midge a few weeks ago, and she looks like a different person. She's happy with new friends and a new dog, too." One of the shelter's first surrenders had been a senior terrier who wanted a nice human to snuggle with. Midge, apparently having been left alone in the old Pembroke Manor as it slowly rotted around her, had fallen in love the second she met the dog.

"You've been to see my sister? You gave my sister a *dog*?"

"Apparently more recently than you have. Mr. Pembroke, you have your answer. The building is not for sale."

Silence.

"You're going to regret this."

Davida hung up. "Probably." She noticed her hands were shaking. "Nikki?"

Crap. It was after five. "Come on, kitty. I need caffeine."

CHAPTER TWO

Beans and Briars was conveniently located between Pembroke Manor and Harbor View Apartments, the somewhat misleadingly named block of redbrick flats Davida called home.

Wednesday night was quiet. No live music or soulful poetry reading was occurring in the warm, homey beanery. "Hi, Lily."

"Hey, girl. Decaf?"

"Not this time. Give me something strong but sweet." Davida made her way to the counter, nodding at a few older ladies sitting at a table with their book club selections in front of them. She hoped they wouldn't notice her shoulder bag had a passenger.

Lily laughed at her order, her freckled face lighting up mischievously. "Strong and sweet? Are you talking about a date for the gala or a cup of coffee?"

"Well, I need both, but I'll take the coffee for now," she chuckled. Dropping her voice, she leaned closer, "If you promise you won't rat me out, I'll show you the next viral Vid-Up star."

Lily suppressed a squeal, her hazel eyes wide as she leaned over the counter. Davida opened the bag and Sparkler's tail popped out first, followed by a shuffle before two black and white ears peeped over the edge of the bag.

"Oh my gosh. He's adorable. I saw his video. I wish I could afford to do a big splashy donation."

"Are you kidding? You locals are doing an amazing job donating your time and effort. Let the rich out-of-towners worry about dropping a grand." Davida put her bag on the scuffed wooden counter and let Lily reach out and give Sparkler a tummy rub, hoping that no one would wonder why the barista appeared to be searching inside her bag.

"I'm still going to be there to help. I've asked Joey and Becca to do the buffet, then help serve champagne. They're both able to make it and they're volunteering their time."

"That's amazing! Thank you so much! I hope no one thinks a buffet is tacky at a hundred bucks a head, but we've got live music, champagne, great food, a gorgeous setting, and a cute kitten. It's for charity. We said it was for charity. People who give $500.00 or more get their names on a plaque as a Paws and Prohibition Donor. I hope that makes the pot sweet enough." Davida tucked the kitten under the canvas flap of her bag and left her hand inside. Nibbling teeth skirted over her knuckles, followed by a tiny rough tongue.

"Yes, it's fine! When you pay that much for dinner at an animal shelter, you know not to expect caviar. Calm down. I never saw you look so rattled, not even when Mr. Herman gave you that 'fat ferret' that turned out to be a pregnant possum."

She sighed, trying to will herself to relax. "Thanks, Lil. Right, it's going to be a busy night. I'm going to leave my taste buds in your hands. Give me something that'll keep me awake but not make me miserable. To go, please."

"Sure thing. Just a minute. Naveen? Black, two sugars, and a pecan roll! Hey, Joey, give Davida a Moonlight in Maine special, to go!"

"Naveen?" Davida turned, eyes narrowing as she took in the dimly lit corners of the coffee shop. Briarwood wasn't a huge town, and it wasn't high on the list of Maine sightseeing tours. Davida supposed there could be a Naveen in town, but she'd never heard that name mentioned locally.

A tall man with thick, curling black hair and caramel skin was heading toward the counter, his eyes locked on hers. "Davida Maxwell?" he said.

"Are you Dr. Northrup?"

"Yes!" He stuck out his hand, his face relaxing. "When I heard the name Davida..."

"Oh, I know. The name Naveen isn't the most common around here." She gestured toward Briarwood as a whole.

"I heard you talking about the fundraiser."

"Right. I thought you weren't arriving until the third."

"Do you two know each other?" Lily called.

"Lily, Naveen Northrup is going to be the vet for the shelter. We've talked on the phone, but we've never met in person."

"Pleased to meet you, Davida-in-person. Yes, I just arrived in town. I have to set up my flat, get the New Year's holiday out of the way, and take care of a few other matters before I start."

"Naturally. It was silly of me to think you'd just magically land here the morning you start work. Of course, you'd have to move in, get settled. Uh—your application mentioned you went to University of Pennsylvania and worked at the Equine Center down there?"

"Yes, for my graduate studies. Before that, I studied veterinary medicine in Birmingham."

"Alabama?" Lily chimed in, pushing a steaming mug and a plate with a golden, pecan-studded sticky roll at the vet.

"Birmingham in England. My parents live there."

"Good gosh. What are you doing all the way over here?" Lily demanded as Naveen paid her.

"Being an eternal disappointment."

"Ooh. I can relate. Lily, change my order from to-go to staying right here."

"I OBSERVED YOUR STOWAWAY," Naveen chuckled as they returned to his table, ensconced in the corner by a pinging steel radiator.

"This is Sparkler. He gets out of any cage I have at the shelter. He's a people cat." Davida dropped her sweater over her lap and let the kitten crawl into it. She hoped that would keep any sharp-eyed patrons quiet. "Well, here's to the first cup of a coffee with a co-worker."

"Cheers." Naveen smiled and tapped his mug to hers.

I love his accent. Davida knew better than to say that aloud, but it didn't stop her from wishing he would keep talking. "The pecan rolls are amazing here. You'll love them."

"Thanks for the tip. I have a bit of a sweet tooth, and this place is almost exactly in the middle of my commute."

The middle of his commute? This place is in the middle of my commute. It's a small town, but still...That would be too crazy. But what are the odds that I'd meet him here, out of all the hours in a day to stop at this little shop? I never get coffee on a Wednesday night. "You don't live at Harbor View, do you?"

Naveen put down his roll without taking a bite. "I just moved in this morning. I'm in 2-C."

"I'm in 1-B!" Davida exclaimed. Sparkler rolled onto his back, claws dragging the sweater with him, wrapping it around his fluffy form. As she freed him, Naveen bit into his pastry and moaned in delight.

"It's a small town. Still, what are the odds? Can I ask you a question?" he asked, brushing crumbs from his lip.

Is it 'Want to grab dinner?' "Sure, anything you like."

"Why in the world did they call it Harbor View? You can't see the harbor."

"I know. It's false advertising. On the other hand, it's an old building. Maybe before bigger buildings came along and took over the landscape, you could see Briarwood Harbor."

"Could be."

"So. Ahem." Davida took a sip of Moonlight in Maine. It was coffee blended with hot cocoa, mixed with a shot of chocolate syrup, and topped with a marshmallow, and a cinnamon stick. Not her usual no frills beverage, but she sucked it down, feeling the knots in her neck undo. "What made you want to work at New Hope after working with horses? We're not really set up for large animal care. Although... well, we do have a lot of acreage." *And we'll keep it, even if Mr. Pembroke has a temper tantrum.*

Naveen lost his smile, his hazel eyes grave. "Equine medicine has come a long way. You know, there is so much you can do now to save a horse's life, even if it has a broken leg."

"Yes. Yes, I've heard a lot about new techniques." Well, she'd skimmed a few articles.

"You'd be surprised how many owners still choose to have the horse put down. Simply because it will never run again. It's an animal. It's not the same as a car. I can't believe someone would kill another living thing for no purpose..." He shook his head and pushed his plate away as if the food had suddenly lost its taste. Anyway, I was sick of that end of veterinary practice. I know in many cases it is a mercy to end the suffering of an animal, and when it's truly in the animal's best interest, I've no problem assisting an animal out of its pain. But I've seen too much selfish, thoughtless killing. I looked for no-kill shelters who wanted a vet on staff, and there you were. One of very few, I might add."

"I can't take all the credit. That's New Hope's idea, I just run with it. But your parents were disappointed, huh? They wanted you to be a big shot racehorse vet or something?"

"They wanted me to be some kind of 'people doctor' or something. British dad. Indian mum. He's a GP. She's a dentist." Naveen shrugged. "They'll come around. I've always liked animals better than people. When I was little, I offered to trade my baby sister for the neighbor's new puppy."

She laughed, which would have been lovely—without the marshmallow in her mouth. One coughing fit later, and she decided that Naveen would have made a great doctor. He had a very good bedside manner, calmly mopping up coffee and retrieving Sparkler from the potted ficus where he had run once his cozy human couch had started convulsing. "I'm really sorry. I hope your parents were able to stop that trade from going through."

"They were. I wasn't very pleased about it at the time. What about you? You mentioned you could relate to disappointing one's parents."

"Let's see. For one thing, I'm almost thirty, with no ring, and no grandbabies. For another thing, I was a pre-law and business dual major at Boston University. I got a scholarship to continue at Columbia. Instead, I took a summer job in the nonprofit sector and never went back. I worked at the original New Hope shelter in New Jersey." Davida moved so that her thick, wavy brown hair fell over her forehead and partially hid her face, embarrassed by the way her eyes immediately teared up whenever she thought about that first summer experience. "I saw three legged cats that were left to die, little mutts that had been used as 'training dummies' for dog fights, dogs that had been starved, burned... Every other shelter in the world would have probably decided it was kinder to put them down. I saw how just a month or two could make the biggest difference. Miracles. Just by not giving up."

Naveen was quiet for a moment. "You have a gala coming up tomorrow?"

"Friday, New Year's. Just about forty-eight hours." She glanced at her watch. How was it almost eight? What happened to a ten-minute coffee break and back to work?

"You should tell that story at the fundraiser. And have a lock box for donations near some cute animals."

"I think Sparkler will be there. Um. You're welcome to come. You're not officially on the clock until Monday, but I hope you'll stop by if you're free." When Naveen nodded, her enthusiasm kicked up another notch. "Have you been past Pembroke Manor yet? It's gorgeous. We're keeping the main rooms as offices and a place for fundraising, but all of the side rooms and the second floor will be for the animals. Oh, and the old garage, which is the size of an apartment. But you should see it. This place has a big, fancy ballroom. Legit, a *ballroom*."

"And that screamed animal shelter to you?" Naveen asked, arching one eyebrow.

Davida shrugged. "After working with New Hope, everything screams animal shelter to me. It's like a way of life."

"Seems like a pretty good one. I'll stop by soon and get the grand tour?"

"Perfect. Oh, and if you do want to come to the gala, the theme is 1920s. The Great Gatsby, flappers, Prohibition Era, and all that stuff. Black tie is acceptable if you don't have something that matches the theme."

"That's pretty fancy for this little place, isn't it?" Naveen looked around the shop and out into the street.

Davida followed his gaze. Snow was flurrying softly, coating the sidewalk and streetlamps with a fluffy layer of white. "Oh, it's a small town, you're right."

"Small? This seems like a hick town, no offense."

Offense taken, Davida thought. "You just got here. Also, my guest list isn't so much for the locals, but the people with money to burn who want to splash out on a fancy costume and drink champagne. I've got a few dozen coming from Portland and Boston. I even have a few coming from Cape Cod."

Naveen nodded, a thoughtful frown on his face. "They're making donations in person? That night?"

"Yep. We have a press photographer coming, and one of the locals is taking shots for our Wall of Wags. With a few big donations, we'll be set up for the year."

"What kind of security do you have for the event?" The handsome vet leaned back in his chair, hazel eyes half-lidded and appraising.

Is he appraising me, or my knowledge of how to hold a swanky fundraiser? He worked with horse people. Horse people always have big fundraisers. Hunt balls. Polo ponies. Horse shows. Well, of course, owning a horse is ten times more expensive than owning a dog, probably more. "Security? Well, all the donations are going to be put into a locked box that's in full view of the room. Oh, and the coats and purses will be in one of the restored rooms that's manned by Lori, one of our volunteers, but there are back-up volunteers to relieve her, so nothing is going to be left unattended. I'm not too concerned about a security risk there. She is a children's pediatrician with a passion for fostering senior rescue dogs and cats. She's treated ninety-five percent of the people in this *hick town*." Davida crooked her fingers in exaggerated air quotes.

Naveen dropped his gaze back to his cup, stirring the dregs vigorously. Davida took that as a good sign. *At least he can catch a hint.* Briarwood wasn't her hometown, but it was her shelter's hometown, and that counted for something.

"It sounds like a lot of people in town are interested in the shelter. That's good. A community that's invested is a bonus."

"Agreed. The next nearest shelter is in Portland, which isn't exactly close. There's a huge feral cat colony in the woods. Plenty of stray cats by the harbor, too. You don't want people to start complaining about property values and taking matters into their own hands." Davida knew it was silly, but she wrapped her hands protectively over Sparkler's ears and whispered, "That's when people start trapping feral cats themselves. Let's just say they're not taking them home to clean them up and give them a good meal."

Naveen shook his head and clucked his tongue in disgust. "The way humans can treat other living creatures shocks me. Even those who are helpless."

"*Especially* those who are helpless," agreed Davida. She thought of Midge Pembroke and the way her faded blue eyes had seemed to drift nervously around the realtor's office, the way her bombastic brother, Preston Pembroke, had urged her to hurry up and sign so that he could make it to his next appointment. Davida remembered her last visit with Midge, just a couple of weeks ago. The woman seemed to have new life and radiance about her, just from being around other people who treated her with kindness. That, and the fact that she had a dog to love and look after as well. "Some people are just jerks," she murmured.

Realizing that Sparkler's presence was becoming noticeable, Davida drained the remnants of her sugary drink to the tune of Sparkler's loud meowing. "I'd better go. I'll be working every minute until the party is over." She rose, breathlessly collecting her coat, scarf, and cat.

"Ah. Yes." Naveen rose as well, awkwardly shifting from foot to foot. Finally, he reached out and took the kitten so Davida could put her other arm in the sleeve of her winter coat. "I could use a break from unpacking. Do you have time to give me a quick tour of the facility tonight? Maybe I'll find a way to be useful."

Davida pulled the zipper up to her chin. She didn't really have time for a tour right now, but if she could put Naveen to work... She could use every pair of hands (or even paws) possible. "I'd be glad to have a little extra help. Bear in mind, what you see is a 'rough draft' of the project. Pembroke Manor is going to be amazing once the renovations are finished. Right now, it's barely up to code."

"Sounds charming." Naveen wrinkled his nose.

Davida busied herself with leaving a tip, scraping several dollars in quarters out of her cat-ears change purse. It was a shame that even the disgusted look on his face didn't change how handsome the veterinarian was. Why were the hot guys always smug jerks?

Of course, he *was* interested in working for the shelter, even though it was hardly a dream job, and he wanted to help animals. Maybe Naveen just had some jerkish tendencies. Davida hoped that those tendencies would dissipate as he got to know her and saw what a lovely town Briarwood could be.

CHAPTER THREE

"This is a magnificent room! It could be a film set."

Even Mr. McSmug couldn't stop turning around in the ballroom, gawping at the ornate chandeliers and the patterns in the hardwood floors, geometric shapes shining like chocolate diamonds under the twinkling overhead lights. His arms were spread out to the side as he turned in an incredulous circle, taking it all in. "This shouldn't have been sold to an animal shelter," he finally said.

"What?" Davida squawked. *Nope. He's definitely a jerk.*

"Look at it! This is supposed to be a ballroom. What are you going to do, have cats and dogs in here for dancing lessons? It's gorgeous, far too gorgeous for a bunch of smelly strays to track it up with muddy feet."

"The ballroom will be for functions. The other rooms are for the animals and day-to-day operations. Come on. I'll show you where the clinic will go. Oh, and you know outside patients can come to you, right? It's not just for New Hope animals. Anyone with a pet can see you, but you have to keep track of which supplies you use for what. Submit a list of what you use on shelter animals for restocking."

"I did read my contract carefully. You didn't honestly think a vet would take the indecent wages you were offering without some sort of loophole, did you?"

If you can't say anything nice, don't say anything at all. Davida mentally repeated the childhood mantra her mother had drummed into her as she led Naveen to what was once the family parlor. Now it was stripped bare of the dusty drapes and thick, stained carpeting, replaced with laminate floor, a steel table, and a bunch of boxes labeled "vet stuff."

"Where does my receptionist sit?" Naveen asked. "This is the exam room. Where would clients wait?"

"One, I'm the receptionist. I'll reserve certain hours for you to take care of New Hope animals, and certain hours will be for private, for-pay patients. You give me the schedule. I'll keep it. I'm very organized."

He gave her an openly disbelieving look.

"What? You don't think I'm organized? I was pre-law and a member of the debate team, the all-campus choir. I managed—"

"There's a cat over your head." Naveen pointed above her head.

"What? Oh. Sparkler! Come down, kitty." Davida blushed and hoped he would think it was just because she was getting warm, still bundled up as she gave him a tour. Sparkler was prowling along one of the exposed beams in the ceiling. "Do you like the beams uncovered? Some people like it. We can cover it."

"Industrial chic meets Tudor, England. Why not?" Naveen groaned and dragged over the rolling exam table. "Hold this."

"Hold the table?"

"Yes." Without further explanation, he grunted and swung his leg onto the gleaming steel surface. With a jump, he was on his feet, tight blue-black jeans and brown brushed wool jacket inches from her face. He smirked down at her and then stretched his arms to the ceiling. "Come here, little one. You can come visit my office another day."

A fleck of melted snow glistened in his hair as he dropped back to the floor, Sparkler purring in the crook of his elbow. "Your cat, miss." He gave her a playful salute and suddenly all Davida could think of were the Hallmark holiday movies where handsome men single-handedly save the widow's ranch at Christmas.

"The dining room can be the waiting room, if you want," she blurted, pointing to a room across the hall.

"That'll work. And the kennels? Isn't there a cattery where this little miscreant should be?" He poked Sparkler's puffy tail tip as it flicked restlessly against her wrist.

"Believe me, I've tried. He seems to have an uncanny knack for opening catches and doors. I tried a padlock, and he managed to stuff a cat toy into the gap where the door meets the base. He shimmied through the opening after I left for the night. Thank God he didn't get his head stuck."

"Well, you'd best make sure he's secure on the night of the party. I don't want cat hair in the canapes."

"Nikki—oh, you'll meet her soon, she's my second-in-command, so to speak—suggested Sparkler come to the party in one of our adoption-event cages. It's three tiers and he'll have lots of room to play. Plus, people will come and coo at him all night." Davida motioned Naveen to follow her down the freshly painted hallway. "I think he only gets out so he can be with humans. Maybe if we had more cats..."

"What is our current status?"

"You mean how many dogs and cats?" Davida couldn't help but like the way he said "our current status." Naveen was clearly taking some ownership.

Wait. That could be good or bad. Do you want Mr. Hot-but-Insulting in charge?

"We have ten older dogs, a few young adult dogs, all large breeds, and one kitten. We had two senior cats that are currently placed with Dr. Lori for fostering. I strongly suspect that might be their purrr-ever home."

Naveen groaned. "Nowhere in my contract did it say I would make terrible animal puns. I'm just establishing that."

Davida quickened her steps. "Come on. This hallway will be sealed off the night of the New Year's Eve party. The other wing, with the entrance hall, ballroom, kitchen, and bathrooms will be in use that night."

"Right. Well. I'd better not keep you. I have to unpack a few dozen boxes if I have any hope of getting a good night's sleep."

"Are you a creature of habit?"

He paused. "Everywhere but work. Animals require a certain understanding and flexibility that precludes a rigid schedule."

Manners escaped her, clearly having taken lessons from the kitten now streaking around the echoing foyer. "I can't tell if you're a jerk or a snob, but either way, it doesn't matter. As long as you take care of sick and injured animals, you're welcome here."

Naveen let out a single, gasping bray of laughter. "What? Did you just call me a snob? Or a jerk?"

"I think honesty between co-workers is valuable." Davida shrugged. "So to clarify, I did *not* call you a snob or a jerk. I said I can't *tell* if you are one."

For the first time, Naveen looked ill-at-ease and lost for words. "I think it's called relating to animals better than people," he finally confessed, forcing a smile on his face.

She softened. "I get that. A lot."

"In my family, you get a very tough skin. You also have to act absolutely assured and confident at all times, because someone will be busy telling you that you're doing it wrong. That you're failing and letting them down." Naveen gave her a smile, a real smile, small and crooked. "It's only by plowing ahead that you get past their objections."

"Again, I get that."

In silence, they walked out of the manor. Davida locked the door behind them. They stood in the frosty night, staring at the garage-slash-office-slash-kennel. "Um. Want to come meet some dogs?"

"Absolutely."

"DAVIDA? DAVIDA? *Vida*!"

"Two cups of wet food to one cup of dry!" Davida jerked awake and sat up, blinking at the overhead lights. Her throat felt dry and her face felt wet. "Oh, ick."

Nikki shook her head as she gently detached a dog food coupon from her boss's face. "Did you sleep at your desk?"

"Did I?" Davida looked around the room. "Ah. Yes, apparently." Her eyes widened. "Where's Sparkler?"

"He was sleeping on top of your head. He jumped up when I came in. Little Boo was ready to defend you with all three pounds of his life," Nikki laughed. "Once he realized it was me, he started crying for his Friskies. Who gets two cups of dry and one cup of wet?"

"The other way around. Duke, the sweet old Rottie with the broken teeth and the gum infection. Naveen said that'll help him keep his weight up while his gums heal."

"Yeah, well, he was underweight to begin with. I think adding a little more dry food would—hey. Naveen? Who is Naveen?"

"The vet. He just got into town and stopped by to see the place last night." Davida stretched and rose, pushing her hair out of her eyes. It felt like there was a flat wasteland in the middle of her scalp—probably where the kitten had slept. She refrained from telling Nikki about her impromptu coffee shop snack with the handsome vet, or the fact that she found him both intriguing and irritating.

"Aww, nice. Is he interested in coming to the gala?" Nikki asked, giving her the side eye as she piled her braids back into a thick, coiled ponytail.

"You mean, is he coming so you don't have to feel as guilty about abandoning me for your college ex? Yes. He might stop by."

"Good." Nikki came over to the desk and stared at the still open laptop. The screen was black at the moment, but Nikki tapped it with a newly manicured nail. "I saw your post on Vid-Up last night. The mayor commented and posted about the gala. Did you see he put up a video about his matching challenge?"

"What? No!" Davida forgot her protesting bladder and made a sharp U-turn back to her desk. "What did he say?"

"Something about how he would ask for the total at eleven o'clock and then match it before midnight."

Davida sat down heavily on the nearest surface, earning a high-pitched shriek as she flattened a rubber chew-toy squirrel. "Match it? Like a one-hundred percent match? As in *double* the total?"

Nikki shrugged, scrolling through her phone as she propped her hip against the desk. "Uhhh—yep. That's what he said. He posted it at midnight last night. I guess you were already asleep, using your laptop for a pillow. Girl, do you not know the meaning of 'work-life balance'?"

"Nope." Davida forced herself up, her knees shaking and her bladder sending up danger signals. "I gotta run."

"Wait, wait! Before you dash off to make yourself presentable, which dress? The pink or the silver?" Nikki chased after her, phone outstretched.

"Whatever matches your nails. Move, unless you want to clean up another puddle."

Davida, making a quick pit stop at home, froze in place as she answered the phone. "Naveen?"

"The snobby jerk you hired. Yes."

"I FOLLOWED THE SHELTER'S Vid-Up channel."

Davida groaned and closed her eyes. Yes, last night did really happen. "Oh, man. I'm sorry about that. I didn't mean—"

Naveen laughed softly. "Yes, you did. But I saw the mayor's comment under your post with Sparkler. It looks like you're going to do it. This Paws and Prohibition stunt is going to work."

Davida prickled like the end of Sparkler's tail. "Stunt!"

"You know what I mean. I couldn't help overhearing your conversation last night. You have servers set up. You have the coat check lady. What you need is a co-host. If I'm the face of the medical end of the shelter, I think I ought to be there."

"Well, you're invited."

"Call me snobby, but I don't want to be another blend-into-the-background guest. You mentioned your assistant wasn't going to be there. What was she going to do?"

Davida frowned as she finished brushing out her hair and draining her orange juice. Had she mentioned that? A few fitful hours of sleep on a desk with a cat nightcap hadn't really improved her mental function. She couldn't remember. Not only that, but she'd forgotten that Naveen was now her neighbor. He could be speaking to her from a few feet away. He could show up and knock on her door any second.

"I need lipstick," she said aloud.

"Well... I've never shopped for it before, but I presume you could tell me what shade to buy? What else would she do?"

"Huh? Oh, no. I didn't mean Nikki would buy me lipstick. I need to get some—uh—before the gala." Before you bump into me in the lobby, looking like a short cross between Paul Bunyan and a bad wig.

"You sound tired." Naveen's voice was accusatory, as if he associated her exhaustion with poor performance.

"I am just a little stressed." Davida crossed her fingers as she popped her multivitamins. "Look, all Nikki was going to do was mingle and shmooze. She'd get people talking, laughing, and dancing. Nikki's local and the life of any party. You're a relative stranger and no offense, the 'hicks' in the town aren't going to respond well to some guy who comes in ready to look down on them."

"Ah. Well, tomorrow night is the night when I get to prove that I don't care if they sit around wearing plaid, whittling walking sticks in the backwoods with their pet lobsters, as long as they let *me* take care of their cats and dogs. And, lobsters, if I must."

"You have *no* idea about living in Maine, do you?" Davida asked, aghast.

"Bad description of the locals?"

"To put it mildly. Look, put all your preconceived notions behind you, rent a tux, and come prepared with your funniest and most moving animal stories. I'll see you at seven tomorrow. If you're 'co-hosting' you can help set up." Davida pulled out her coat, stepped into her boots, and said a little prayer as she looked out at the lowering clouds. Please, no Nor'easters until next week! Ha. Next year. She shivered, not from the cold, but from the sudden realization that in twenty-four hours, she could set the shelter up to save animals for the entire year. Or, she could put them on a rocky path where they would struggle,

Nikki would quit to find a better job, and Naveen would be fully justified in giving her superior looks.

"Sounds good. Just one question."

"Yes?"

"Should the tux be plaid?"

Davida hung up. But despite her mounting exasperation, she had to laugh.

CHAPTER FOUR

Nikki sashayed through the office in a tight pink dress that shimmered as the light caught the scalloping sequins across it. It perfectly matched the powder puff pink shade of her nails and complemented the silver of her ridiculously high heels. Davida stared up at the statuesque woman made even more so by her fancy footwear.

"Are you sure you're not secretly the entertainment for tonight?" Davida asked.

"What do you mean?" Nikki demanded, hands on curvaceous hips.

"I mean you look like you're ready to take to the stage. If you were trying to catch John's eye, you have succeeded." Davida teasingly fanned herself. "Too hot to handle, hot mama."

"Oh my gosh, I really hope so. He's sending a car for me, can you believe it?"

"Well, he must really want you there." Davida gave her assistant a grudging smile. She would have felt so much better if Nikki were the one going to be by her side tonight. Even though she tried to appear confident, Davida was nervous about hosting a ballroom full of relative strangers and trying to convince them to empty their wallets. Her uncle had strong opinions that lawyers were all blood-sucking, money grubbing leeches, but she felt awkward even *discussing* money. Even though it was for charity, she still felt uneasy. That was something New Hope had told her she'd better get over since donations kept the shelters afloat.

Remember, you're not asking for you, her mentor had advised her, you are asking for the cats and dogs because they have no voice.

"You need to be a voice for the voiceless. Pro bono work. Voice for the voiceless. I got this," she muttered as Nikki took one more selfie and texted it to John.

"What did you say, Dav?" Nikki turned around and her eyes widened. "Davida Maxwell, you aren't even dressed. Do not tell me that you are wearing that ratty black sweater and that pair of pants!"

"You know I'm not," Davida reassured her, shaking out her hair and standing. "I have my shiny black flapper get-up hanging in the closet. I'm going to get changed before the party starts but after the caterers and the band get set up. We're so lucky we got Luke and the Blue Moose Brothers to play for such a low price. By low I mean—for food and drinks."

Nikki nodded and checked the time on her phone once more. "Everybody in Briarwood loves them. They'll keep the joint jumping and they are definitely going to channel that Roaring Twenties style."

As Davida opened her mouth to ask for more tips to charm the locals, a car horn beeped twice from Pembroke's long driveway. "Oh, that's the driver!" Nikki squealed. "Text me how it goes. Keep updating social media. Don't forget to work the cat and dogs into the show whenever you can."

"Work them in?" Davida protested trotting after Nikki. "What am I supposed to do? Get everybody in their tuxes down to scoop poop in the kennel?"

"You'll think of something." Nikki waved over her shoulder. With a glitter of pink and silver, she disappeared into a black Cadillac.

Davida turned back to the empty office. Sparkler was sleeping in the entryway so she supposed technically it wasn't empty. "Come on, Sparkler. It's just you, me, and a to-do list that's two miles long until Naveen shows up."

But Davida soon found that the hours she was dreading didn't drag by. The to-do list kept her busy, and helping the night's entertainment and volunteer staff get set up filled the time. It was 7:45 when she took a quick scrub in the utility sink in the corner of the kennel and slipped into her short black dress covered in swinging fringe. She brushed her dark curls into smooth waves, and to complete the ensemble, she fastened a black beaded band topped with a curled white ostrich feather around her hair. She would be the first to admit that she was rather short and a little too padded in the hips, but the dress made her feel sexy.

That's good, Davida thought, nodding to herself. "Sexy means confidence, confidence means you sound like you know what you're doing, and people will invest in you if they believe you. Now, please don't let me say anything stupid or tacky when Naveen gets here. I don't need to have a verbal sparring match that pokes holes in my little bubble of calm."

As if on cue, Naveen popped his head through the front door to the office. "Davida? I wasn't sure whether I should go up to the main house or—" The vet trailed off and swallowed a few times.

Davida smiled, hoping he hadn't heard her speaking right before he poked his head in. "No, it's perfect that you're here. I have the lock box and a few things to carry up. Why don't you come in out of the cold—before we go back out into the cold?" she concluded lamely.

"I don't officially start working for you for a few more days." Naveen stepped through the door and brushed snow off of the immaculate black velveteen collar of his long winter dress coat that came just to his knees.

Davida rolled her eyes and huffed, "Geez, you don't have to carry the lock box. You can just take the business cards."

"I wasn't objecting to helping. I meant that it wouldn't be out of line for me, a person who is currently a non-co-worker, to tell you that you look absolutely stunning. Like something out of a swanky, smoky 1920s nightclub."

Davida blushed. "Well, that was the idea. My hair didn't want to cooperate, but I don't suppose a girl can have everything in one night."

Naveen put a finger to his lips. "Don't say such things. The fates are listening. You want everything to go well tonight, don't you? I thought this was to set us up for the year?"

Davida blinked a couple of times to make sure her eyes were working. The dim lights, the rakish curl of his thick black bangs, the way he quirked his lips when he shushed her... It had to be an illusion. Too perfect. Too handsome. Too *here*, darn it. Davida had to fight for everything she'd ever had, take risks that only paid off at the eleventh hour. Fate wouldn't drop a handsome, compassionate vet (with a few quirks, okay) in her proverbial lap. "I want everything to go well," she finally croaked.

"Excellent. Me, too. Let me carry that," Naveen took the heavy wooden lock box from her, looking critically at its ornate mahogany scrolls and whorls. "This is a masterpiece of craftsmanship. It looks like it came right from the time period, too."

"You won't believe it. Jilly Strache—her mom owns the antique store— gave it to Nikki yesterday. Much better than the ugly black metal thing I got from the office supply store. It looks good and sturdy, too." Davida looked at the box with a critical eye. She was sure she had seen this unique pattern of carved roses and briars somewhere before. "It's hand carved and the wood looks like it's several inches thick. No one could possibly get into that without her heck of a racket, that's for sure."

"I'd say that it's a genuine antique, too. You say someone simply donated it for the sake of this part? It's amazing how invested people are in this little shelter." Naveen shook his head, marveling.

Davida knew she shouldn't gossip, but her tongue was tempted to wag like a dog's tail. As they walked up the frosty driveway to the manor house she confessed, "A little bit of it might have something to do with the way the Pembroke family treated this place. The past generations poured money into the local economy, but Preston Pembroke, the current family patriarch, isn't really the kind of local native son the people of Briarwood are proud of."

"Oh?" Naveen raised one eyebrow.

Again, Davida thought that it wasn't fair that he should look so handsome just by moving one muscle on his face. "I'm an outsider myself, but from what I know it seems like the people of Briarwood work hard and work together. This town has been around since the early 1700s. In its earliest days, it was just a fishing and trading outpost surrounded by wild blackberry bushes. A lot of the townsfolk have links to indigenous tribes. The Pembrokes were outsiders. The *first* Mr. Pembroke came from England and married the daughter of a wealthy New York tycoon. They built the big mansion over here in 1920. They didn't ingratiate themselves with the locals, but they sure knew how to throw a party and pump money into the town. For that, people came to accept them and their son, Frederick."

"It's amazing what money and a little alcohol will do to people." Naveen nodded, chuckling as they crunched along the path.

Davida quickened her steps. The first early arrivals would be coming in a matter of minutes. Naveen easily stretched his long legs to keep pace with her

"So? You said they liked the family. This place was the hot spot. What happened?"

"Well, my sources tell me—"

"Who are your sources?" Naveen interrupted.

Davida resisted the urge to elbow him. "Pretty much anyone who stopped by the house in the last two months, but especially Nikki. She's the only other full-time person besides me. Anyway, people didn't mind the first or second generation, but Frederick and Flora had three kids, and the eldest was Preston. How to put this tactfully?"

"Don't?" Naveen suggested, his eyes twinkling with a hint of naughtiness. "I like my dirt straight, no sugar-coating."

"Then I'll put it this way—Preston acted like his money entitled him to look down on people. He seemed to think that just because his grandparents were from London and New York, and his father had gone to the best schools and made the family fortune even bigger, he could treat the people of Briarwood like they were... I don't know..." She gave Naveen a sidelong glare, "Like they were *hicks*."

"I will never live that down, will I?" he groaned as they stepped on to the wrap-around front patio.

Davida didn't give him the satisfaction of a reply, merely continuing, "I think the final straw for people was when he left his sister here all alone. I mean, it made sense that his brother moved down to Florida with his elderly parents. They needed care, and Midge didn't want to leave. People assumed Preston would do right by her, maybe move into the manor with her or hire live-in help, or visiting companions... something. Instead, it seems that all he did was shunt her off to others to look after. The locals tried to go see her and check in on her, but Midge— Hm. Midge retreated into herself and was too frightened to let people inside to help her. She'd get her grocery order delivered and that was pretty much it."

Naveen clucked his tongue as they stepped into the foyer and shook a light dusting of snow off their coats. "Poor woman."

Davida dropped her voice. People were already milling around. Even though her information was common knowledge, she didn't need anyone thinking she was spilling local secrets to the "outsider." "I wouldn't say that. I think Midge lived in her own world. She thought she could take care of herself because she didn't fully understand the realities of life the way others do. She survived, so I guess she was right about taking care of the basics. It was the house that suffered. She never did any upkeep or maintenance. Preston might have known about the leaks and the repair issues, or he might not. If it cost him money, it wasn't his problem. That's why I got this house so cheap—it was falling apart."

"What a prince." Naveen clicked his tongue in annoyance once more. "I hate when people act like money means more than family. Or status, for that matter. Where do you want this box?"

"Over here against the photo-op wall. I'll show you." Davida walked Naveen through the ballroom to a pedestal flanked by heavy brocade drapes salvaged from the manor. Sparkler was in a three-tiered cage, hopping madly from tier to tear as he chased a catnip toy on a string. The cat would grab hold of the toy and its springy rope would cause it to rebound. Sparkler had attracted a crowd of waiters and caterers, as well as the band. Everyone had stopped setting up and had their phones out, aiming their screens at the adorable kitten celebrity.

"Excuse me," Davida uttered a single phrase and the crowd parted, letting her lead Naveen to the pedestal which was underneath a banner of gold lamé letters that proclaimed *Happy New Year!* Beneath them, glittery red letters formed a second arch that read, *A New Life with New Hope.*

"That's a bit much." Naveen jerked his angular chin toward the lettering.

Davida shrugged. "Listen, I'm the one who studied fundraising and charitable tax donations when I signed up for this franchise. This is what people want. They want to be associated with something positive by name."

Naveen rolled his wrist with a flourish as he bowed low over the box, placing it on the little faux-marble pedestal. "As the flapper queen commands, I shall do. I suppose it's not tacky in the spirit of celebration."

"Thank you. I think." It pays your salary, Davida wanted to snarl, but held her tongue.

"It certainly seems like Squiggles is loving the attention."

"Sparkler." Davida watched the kitten look out of the wire bars of his spacious playground. As the staff moved away, Sparkler mewed after them, no longer content to chase his toy. "You'll have lots of visitors soon, Sparky. Take it easy, okay?"

The kitten mewed piteously, its little white paw reaching out and wrapping over one of Davida's fingers.

"Ohh. Oh, dear. He *is* charming." Naveen wiggled his fingers through the bars and Sparkler immediately rolled over for a belly rub.

"Afraid he'll steal your thunder?" Davida challenged.

Naveen slipped out of his coat, revealing an immaculately cut black suit with a paisley waistcoat underneath, a pocket watch and chain completing the ensemble and giving it that vintage air. "Why, Miss Maxwell. Does that mean you find me charming?"

Why was it suddenly so hard to talk? Her throat felt like she was trying to swallow something sticky and sweet. "I—"

"I need everyone to be quiet! Final mic check!" Luke, the leader of the Blue Moose Brothers Band, hushed their conversation as he adjusted the microphone stand and motioned to the man by the boxy black amps beside him.

"We'd better save that conversation for later," Davida whispered, stepping back and smoothing her dress.

Naveen nodded. He seemed to have an internal struggle before whispering back, "That means there is a conversation you want to have, right?"

She didn't answer, pretending not to hear, and rushing off. She did have a million things to do—and she was noticing a pattern, an annoying one. Naveen liked to have the last word.

That's a problem. So do I.

CHAPTER FIVE

"I think this is going to work. I think this is actually going to work!" Davida helped Dr. Lori hang a luxurious mink stole next to a long evening cape. People were dressed to the nines, coming out in costumes that sparkled and swayed with fringes.

"I've never seen a bunch of these people. I think you were right—those social media posts with Sparkler did the trick. Why, I think as many people have posed with that kitten as they have the mayor or your money box."

"I don't mind. The money box is *stuffed,* and it is only nine-thirty. I already had to shake it down a couple of times. I hope we have room for more donations, or I'm going to have to make a run to the office. I have one of those portable fireproof box safes in there. We can move the cash to that until we can deposit it."

"Well, you'd better make some kind of announcement about the mayor's matching donation. You'll have to count it out before then." Dr. Lori chuckled. "Better yet, let Samuel make it himself. He loves to talk. At least he usually uses that foghorn voice for the good of Briarwood."

Samuel Woodbine, Briarwood's mayor, looked like a cartoon depiction of a millionaire. All that was missing was the monocle and the bags of money with the dollar signs on the front. The portly man with silver hair and a fluffy white mustache was clad in an old-fashioned tailcoat and paisley ascot. He held sway at the donation box, talking up the shelter, talking up the town, and holding Sparkler in one arm like a lady's fur muff.

Holding Sparkler!?

"Sparkler!" Davida took off across the ballroom, dodging trays of champagne and canapes as she skidded on her sexy black heels. "Mr. Woodbine, how did you get the cat out of his cage?"

"Hmm? Oh, Mr. Twinnings, this is Davida Maxwell. She's a real go-getter. She organized this whole shindig and has fixed this eyesore up. It's a real beauty, isn't it? Davida, this is Mr. Twinnings. He's the mayor of Oakdale outside of Portland. They have an animal shelter that's overrun with puppy mill outcasts. I told him you were the lady to talk to."

"I'll be happy to talk to you, Mr. Twinnings, absolutely. We may have room for a few of your occupants. I'll know more on Monday. In the meantime..." Davida held out her hands, wiggling her fingers as she gave the mayor a pointed look. "I know he's a cute photo-op, but I really don't want him to get loose and get hurt. He could get stepped on with all these people dancing the Charleston."

"What's that, Davida? Oh! This little fellow. Well, you know, I didn't let him out. He climbed straight up my tails and perched on my shoulder. Maybe he's part parrot!"

"I'd say part porcupine," Mr. Twinnings laughed. "What a tail he has!"

"Doesn't he, though?" Davida forced a smile and retrieved the cat. She excused herself as another crowd of costumed party goers was ushered to the donation box by a smiling Naveen. Two women in tight dresses, one in scarlet red and the other in emerald green, hung on his arms, leaning on him and laughing up into his face. One went so far as to tangle her fingers, wrapped in silk elbow-length gloves, through his bangs, teasing them into a more rakish curl.

Jealousy flared up through her middle. She told him to shmooze, not seduce.

With a smile that fell short of her eyes, she joined them at the donation box. "Excuse me, Dr. Northrup? Would you help me with our little escapee?"

"Oh my gosh, a kitten! He's so adorable!" Emerald Dress gushed.

"Let me hold him!" Scarlet Dress squealed.

"I'll find you ladies in a little while." Naveen bowed to his companions and to Davida's elbow, steering her back to Sparkler's habitat.

"Wow. A bow and everything. Playing it up, aren't we?"

"I'm sorry, who was the woman perched on the piano singing 'Old Lang Syne' like a smokey-eyed whiskey-voiced temptress?"

Davida blushed. "That was Luke's idea. I like singing. Wait, you think I have smoky eyes? Did you say temptress?"

Naveen made a noise like a blocked kettle through compressed lips. "What's wrong with the cat?"

"He got out! The mayor was holding him. Someone must have unlocked his crate!"

Naveen picked up the padlock. "This is still locked. No scratches. I don't think it's been tampered with. Where's the key?"

Davida drew a long silver chain out from the shoulder-high neckline of her flapper dress. "Trust me, no one's gotten hold of this."

"Then you were right to call him an escapee. Put him back in and we'll watch him this time and see how he manages to worm his way to freedom."

"Shouldn't that be 'cat his way to freedom' instead?"

Naveen groaned again, a high-pitched huff between thinned lips.

"You sound like a teakettle when you do that. One that's broken."

"I'll watch the cat. You mingle." Naveen gave her elbow a firm nudge, and she was glad to take the hint.

BY 10:30, DAVIDA WAS starting to wish she'd worn more comfortable shoes. She hobbled her way toward Luke, planning to take the mic and make the announcement about the 11:00 cut off for donations.

Of course, she couldn't get there that easily. People kept stopping her to tell her what a blast the party was. That was a joy, but it was also throwing off her timing. "Excuse me. Hi! Great to see you! Yes, it is a great party. Hi—"

"Oh, good, it's you. Help me get to the donation box."

Davida stopped in her tracks. It was Andrea Strache, the owner of Briarwood Loft, the town's antique shop. The petite woman was in a floor length dress, but that didn't conceal the enormous gray and black walking cast she was dragging with the help of a fabulously ornamental walking stick. "Andrea! What happened to you?"

"I dropped the tailgate of Denny's trailer on my foot three days ago. But I wasn't going to miss this party. Denny is off ice-fishing with his brother and Jilly's heading back to Portland with her new boyfriend for a long weekend," she grunted. "I know you can't keep them little, but it's hard watching them grow up, especially if you think they're making the wrong choices."

"Oh! I'm sorry Jilly and Denny couldn't come to the party."

"Well, Jilly dropped me off a little while ago, but she wouldn't come in. She said she had to get back to her mystery man."

"She calls her boyfriend a mystery man? And I thought Naveen was pretentious." Fortunately, a wailing jazzy number on the trumpet hid the last bit of her thought.

"I'm sure she doesn't, but she won't tell us who he is." Andrea grimaced, leaning heavily on her walking stick as they made their way to the donation box. "She met him at the bank. She's the vice-president in charge of mortgages now. Well, I think that's what she does. I don't know her actual title. It's vice-something and she handles all of the real estate deals."

"That's amazing. Jilly's about my age, right? That's big for someone so young."

"Well, she's almost thirty. And it's a small bank," Andrea said drily. "Anyway, I don't like this boyfriend. He moves fast, this fellow. They only started seeing each other a few weeks ago. I liked it better when she was working for Woodbine. He was a real family man, and always made sure Jilly had time to pop home for a visit when Denny was having his chemo treatments. Not that I blame the bank for Jilly spending less time with us. I blame the boyfriend. She thinks the sun rises and sets on him. Says he's going places, going to make it to the big time, and she'll be making it with him." Andrea roller her eyes. "One diamond bracelet and he's got her dropping her own mother off to hobble alone on New Year's Eve. I can't drive with the boot yet."

"Do you need a lift home?"

"Oh, Dr. Lori will take me back. Ooh!" Andrea's eyes lit up when she saw the box up close. "Look at this baby! Where'd you get it?"

Davida frowned. "From Jilly. She gave it to Nikki yesterday. Nikki said it was from the antique shop."

Andrea looked at it closely. "It isn't, but I could understand her thinking that. Nikki must've seen the pattern and assumed."

The instinct to defend Nikki was instantaneous, but Davida simply nodded and looked interested. "Oh? Why is that?"

"Being new to these parts, you wouldn't know this. See the design of roses, thorns, and berries carved into the wood? That's what we locals call the Sweetbriar design. It's what you might call a trademark of local carvers. Only a few old timers still make furniture with this design. This is definitely an old piece, though."

"I knew I had seen it before. Oh! When I got this place, there was lots of old furniture left behind. Most of it we had to throw out due to woodworm and mildew, but we kept a few big wardrobes. They had this pattern carved into the edge."

"You have an original Sweetbriar pattern wardrobe storing dog chow and cat kibble somewhere?" Andrea demanded, stuffing a folded check into the slit on the box's lid.

Davida shrugged. "It's better than sitting there empty, gathering dust. Is it valuable?"

"Collectors sure like it. This box would go for a few hundred dollars. The wardrobes might be a grand. Maybe more."

"I'll save that knowledge for emergencies."

"Hey, if you throw a party like this every year, you won't have any emergencies, not the financial kind anyway." Andrea laughed and limped off.

At that moment, Mr. Woodbine made his way back to the lock box again, this time accompanied by a woman wearing a tweedy jacket and carrying a huge camera on her shoulder. "Miss Maxwell, stand with me for a moment. Hold the kitten up to the box while I put in my personal donation." The mayor displayed a large prop check, passing Davida a smaller one. "That's the real one. This is for the photo," he whispered.

"I figured," Davida whispered back, taking the check and a purring Sparkler. "Did Dr. Northrup get him out for you?"

"Oh no. No. I found him eating a piece of salami on the floor by the buffet table."

"I see." Davida looked around, hoping to make eye contact with Naveen. He was supposed to be watching the kitten and preventing his escape!

She glared daggers through the room as the press photographer set up her tripod. At last, her eyes landed on the handsome doctor. He was sandwiched between Emerald Dress and Ruby Dress, looking—miserable. Uncomfortable. Even his to-die-for hair seemed to droop as he forced a laugh.

Darn it. I'm going to have to go rescue him.

"Smile! This is for the front page!" The photographer called.

Everyone on the dance floor paused. Davida and the mayor held up the huge dummy check over the box. Sparkler licked a paw, unconcerned by the sudden snapping of the flashbulb.

"I have to go return this little guy. Would you like to make the announcement, Mayor Woodbine? After all, it is your money."

"I'd be delighted. All donations need to be in by eleven. Goodness, that's in a few minutes."

"Here, put your actual check in," Davida prompted the mayor. She watched him slide the check into a pale blue envelope with the mayoral seal embossed on it, then fold it in half and push it into the box.

"FOLKS! GUESTS! I HAVE an important announcement to make." Mayor Woodbine held sway. The music stopped, but chattering and giggling continued in the background. "Step up, step up, folks! If you have a last-minute donation to make, now is the time. After the clock strikes eleven, you've lost the chance to help New Hope *double* their takings!" Instantly, a line of guests began weaving their way through the crowd, to the box.

It was the perfect cover. Davida slid behind Naveen and his dynamic duo. With a soft tug on his sleeve, she pulled him backward, out of the ballroom, and into the hallway that led to the kitchen and dining room.

"Thank God. I thought I was going to have to marry one to save myself from a lifetime of putting up with *both* of them!" Naveen hissed, sinking back against the wall.

"Not happy with your bevy of beauties?" Davida teased.

"They're insipid, like a pair of fashion magazines with the power of speech. Thank you for the rescue."

"Well, in all honesty, it's a rescue from them, but not from me. You said you would watch Sparkler and find out how he escaped. Once he did it, I didn't expect you to let him go wandering around, eating off the buffet!"

"What?" Naveen seemed to realize for the first time that she had a furry passenger. "I watched him for twenty minutes, being yammered at by Caitlin and Julia the whole time." He shuddered. "I finally told them I needed to get some punch and they followed me."

"Then how did he—"

"It's a matter for further study, but I promise you, I wasn't derelict in my duties."

"Okay, okay, I believe you. Geez, he's fast. I wonder—" Davida stopped speaking as the hallway was plunged into darkness. The ballroom erupted with shrieks and shouts.

She and Naveen stumbled over one another, squashing Sparkler between them. The kitten hissed in protest and dug his needle-like claws into her hip. "Sorry, baby!" she exclaimed.

"It's all right, it's just my ankle." Naveen breathed against her cheek as they tripped over one another and into the pitch-black ballroom.

"I wasn't talking to—never mind." Davida raised her voice as she managed to find her footing. Everyone, remain calm. I'm sure there is a simple solution. Stay still and—" She never finished her sentence. The lights flickered back on.

"Good heavens. I must've blown a fuse. Well, some of my constituents say that I have an electrifying personality." Woodbine laughed at his own joke. "And now... I have one more surprise before midnight. Would everyone join me out by the pond for a New Year's fireworks display? Meanwhile, our gracious hostess can find out just how much you've helped these sweet animals—and how badly you've hurt my bank account."

Naveen shared a smile with her as everyone rushed for their coats and made their way to the manor's sprawling, frosty grounds. "Come on. We'd better help that little old lady with the coat check."

Davida nodded, smiling in return, tension leaving her body. She was surprised when Naveen offered her his elbow. She took it, and somehow, they were leaning together. No, leaning *into* one another. Friends. Companions. Comrades. Maybe something more? Just maybe.

"This is going to be a good year. I can feel it," she sighed.

CHAPTER SIX

"No. This can't be right. Thirty-two thousand-eight-hundred-fifty dollars." Naveen finished totaling the checks.

"Not bad for hicks, right?" Davida chuckled, counting the cash. "Nine-hundred-seventy-five in cash."

"I'll never live that down, will I?"

"No. Well, not for a while. Or until you do something worse that I can tease you about."

"If I started seeing one of the locals, do you think that might help? Even if she's a newcomer? She's been embraced by the locals. And to clarify, my erstwhile admirers are not from around here." Naveen neatly stacked the checks.

"Hmm. It could. But I—wait. No. Oh, God! No!" Davida rocketed up from her seat in the office.

Naveen scooted back from the pile of checks, horrified. "I'm sorry. I'm sorry, forget it."

"Where's the envelope?"

"What envelope?"

"The mayor's envelope!" Davida felt ice water flow through her, completely obliterating the single glass of champagne she'd indulged in.

"Come again?" Naveen cocked his head. "He can't write us a check until we give him the total."

"He already wrote a check! A big, fat, ten-grand check that he put in a pale blue envelope! It has his personal mayoral seal on it. It's got gold letters! It's *fancy*!"

"Sit down. Head between your knees!"

"This is no time for innuendo! But, yes, if I'm not run out of town or imprisoned, I'd love to go out sometime!" Davida shrieked. Overhead fireworks boomed and the sound of whining came from the kennel. "Oh, God, who would do fireworks at an animal shelter?"

"Steady on. You're on the verge of hyperventilating or passing out. Your color is horrible." Naveen put his hands on her shoulders, forcing her back to her seat. "Stay there. I'll go reassure the dogs. Hm. Do you have a radio in here?"

"There's a digital sound system in there. We put it on Calming Classical during the night." Davida put her head in her hands.

"I'm putting it on my own personal Peaceful Pet playlist." Naveen disappeared into the back.

Davida disappeared into a cloud of bleak thoughts.

One night to make this year go smoothly. So far, so good. Ha! She'd earned enough to pay Naveen and Nikki's salaries for several months and keep the shelter going. Doubled? They'd be set for the year. Everyone was raving about the party. She couldn't wait to see what else she could do with the space. What about an Easter Egg hunt in the spring? What about Halloween Trick or Doggy Treat?

None of those things would happen if the mayor's ten-thousand-dollar donation was missing under her watch.

She ignored Naveen's advice and got back to her feet, swaying slightly, head feeling like a boat on rough sea. She opened the wooden lock box again. The envelope wasn't left inside. There were no secret catches or latches, no false bottoms. She dug her fingers around the edges as Sparkler pawed her leg, wanting to get into her lap.

"You can see in the dark. You can get into any room and out of any cage. You could tell me what happened, I bet."

Naveen returned. "What could have happened?"

"People will assume I skimmed off the top. I can't even hide it, not that I would. The mayor would know from looking at his accounts."

"Not necessarily. The mayor will know the money leaves his account... he'll expect that. But a thief would simply put the money in their own pockets. And if it's a thief... why not steal the cash?"

"Maybe they did. We don't know how much was in here," Davida mumbled, head drooping.

"No, no. Why not take *all* the cash? Why not take the whole box, cash, checks, and all? This had to happen very quickly, and most likely when the lights went off, yes?"

"Yes." There was a note of questioning in her voice.

"So, the person probably had two minutes, tops. In the dark, the person could have grabbed a handful of cash and checks..." Naveen trailed off, frowning.

"If they took a random bunch of cash and checks, we'd never know. Taking the mayor's check would be instantly noticeable."

"Which means they *want* someone to find out. What thief wants to be caught?"

"Not a smart one," Davida muttered bitterly. "Why do this to us? To these poor animals?"

"That's it! That's it, exactly."

"What's it?" Davida felt like she was moving in a fog. Words didn't make sense.

Naveen's brown eyes were locked on hers. "Someone wants to ruin this night. They probably took the only check that couldn't be 'misplaced' or 'miscounted.' Why? To make sure that the shelter is rocked by scandal."

"It'll shut down without the town behind it." Davida rubbed at her eyes. She would not cry. Crying wouldn't help.

"Who wants this place shut down?" Naveen pressed.

"No one! You can see that! Everyone here loves this place. Like I said, the town was happy someone saved Pembroke Manor. They liked that Midge Pembroke was finally in a safe environment. The mayor, the press, the locals... This is ideal. Too good to fail." Davida choked down a sob. "That's what they said about the Titanic, isn't it?"

HE PACED. SHE ROCKED. Sparkler shed all over her black dress. Outside, a loud volley of pops and bangs heralded the finale of the fireworks.

"Someone from the outside then!" Naveen rounded on her and slammed his hands on the desk.

"What?"

"Someone from the outside. Not local. Who could want you to fail? Or the shelter?"

"I just told you—" Davida hesitated. "Well... there is one person. But he's not here. Preston Pembroke. The oldest son of the Pembroke family. He's not local. He lives near Portland, I think. His sister Midge had this house, but she wasn't competent to run it alone. I believe she always had some cognitive issues, but now they've been compounded by early onset dementia or something similar, and she really needed to be looked after. Preston pressured her to leave the place and sell it cheap, to me. He didn't get any money off of it. The assisted living place takes a person's assets to pay for their long-term care. It's actually a good deal in Midge's case. She's much younger than most residents. I went to visit her a few times."

Naveen stared at her, head cocked in confusion. "Does he want her to have the house back? Was he mad that she sold it?"

"He pressured her into selling it," Davida reiterated, joining him in his pacing. "But he called me this week. He offered me fifty percent over my purchase price if I would sell it back to him. He wants to turn it into a factory. Oh, that's how they made their money. Frozen foods."

"Call the police! This man must be—"

Davida held up her hand. "Here. The man must be *here* to steal an envelope containing a ten-thousand-dollar check. He's not. Preston Pembroke is super well-known in the area. He's also ~~not~~ a hard person to miss. Discreet doesn't describe him. If he were here, we'd know. As for calling the police, that won't be necessary. The sheriff is already here. He's the guy who looks like he wants to be Zorro." Davida winced at the memory of the pot-bellied man in black, who had pointed out that the original Zorro had come out in 1920, so he was on-theme.

"So this Pembroke isn't on the premises. What about some associate of his?"

"No one in town would help him, not any one I can think of. Certainly not anyone here tonight."

"Okay. Well..." Naveen steepled his fingers under his chin, eyes heavenward. "There are people here you don't know. I'm not simply speaking of the locals that you've not met, but there are strangers here. Strangers from out of town. Hm. If you had stolen a check, what would you want to do with it?"

"Cash it."

"You are not helping your case." Naveen shrugged impatiently and took off his jacket.

Davida watched him pace in his shirt sleeves and fitted vest, intelligent face a mask of concentration. "If I had stolen a check, I'd want it for the money. If I stole it to put a monkey wrench in things, to discredit the shelter and the person running it—I'd want it hidden. I'd want it far, far off the property and off my person, so no one could find it before the crisis happened. I wouldn't want it associated with me."

"But at the same time, you don't want it left lying just anywhere. If someone finds it, or someone finds evidence it was destroyed, there goes your plan."

She tapped her fingers against her lower lip. "If the theft was discovered—which they would want it to be or else the whole plan to throw the shelter into chaos goes up in smoke—then the next step is searching people's bags and pockets. Most people would cooperate, so the ones who don't look like they have something to hide."

"Cars. They've got to get it into their car."

"They're all outside now!" Davida wailed.

"By the pond. Not the cars." Naveen snapped his fingers. "That's the opposite end of the grounds, isn't it?"

"Yes. But it's not like we're policing people. Anyone can walk through the grounds or leave when they feel like it."

"Most people aren't, though. The cars are parked by the garage—which is now the kennel and the office. Us. I haven't heard a car start. Have you?"

"There were *fireworks*, Naveen!" Davida growled. Sparkler sat up and stretched, alarmed by his human mother's snarl.

He smirked. "No headlights came on."

"I was counting money. I wasn't watching the window."

"I'm observant. It's a vet thing."

"I'm argumentative. It's a lawyer thing."

"Right now, both of us have 'not-wanting-to-go-to-jail' things! Do you have leashes for the dogs?"

"Huh? Yes. Why?"

"I have an idea. I'll keep people busy by the pond. You keep an eye out in the parking area. Help me leash up the dogs in the kennel."

"What, all of them?" Davida demanded, following Naveen back to the section of the converted garage that currently held their canine visitors.

"We're doing a Midnight Mutt Strut before you announce the total. Even if you don't find the check, we'll tell them the total, just adding $10,000. It'll all work out." Naveen squeezed her hand as he took a bouquet of thick woven leashes from her.

She smiled weakly. At least he'd said 'both of us' when he mentioned being arrested. "You took a deep dive on this job, huh?"

Naveen smiled at her, a real smile, nothing hidden or snarky in it. "It's been enlightening."

CHAPTER SEVEN

Luke and the Blue Moose Brothers were leading the guests in an impromptu conga around the lake. From her location, she could hear the saxophonist adding some fancy trills, hear the drummer smacking the beat on something, and Davida could even make out faint sounds of a strummed guitar. Drunk people were laughing. Dogs were barking. Everyone sounded happy.

"Naveen is rocking it. Too bad he's wrong."

No one had approached the cars. Davida blew on her cold fingers and rocked from foot to foot, wondering how common frostbite was in Maine, and how quickly it could set in.

Something rubbed against her ankles.

"Sparkler! My goodness, cat. How did you get out this time? I'm beginning to think you have supernatural powers. At least you have the sense to stick near people."

As if on cue, the kitten went running off, tail held high and ears pricked forward. "No! Sparkler, wait!" Davida groaned and looked around. Well, no one was in the parking area. She didn't see anyone moving around in front of the manor itself. With a sigh, she chased after the cat as best she could on the uneven ground in her impractical shoes.

DAVIDA DUCKED AS PINE branches whipped across her sides and snagged her hair. She tore off her feathered headband and stuffed it into her coat pocket, trying to keep her squinting eyes on the white beacon of Sparkler's tail.

Eventually, the kitten stopped and disappeared. Davida just stopped, staring.

There was a tiny little shed on the property, a tiny little *pink* shed, like a child's playhouse.

"Oh, this isn't creepy at all," Davida put her hand in her coat pocket and felt for her phone. She turned on the beam of the built-in flashlight and sent Naveen a text.

If I'm not back in ten minutes, you and the sheriff come walk through the woods east of the kennel. There's a pink playhouse. I'm probably about to be sacrificed to demonic puppets or something.

Steeling herself, she walked closer, phone held out, phone setting up to dial 911 if needed.

"—as much as dogs, but I still like kittens. I had a kitten once. Now I have a dog. I love my dog."

Davida's heart sank. She knew that voice.

Midge Pembroke.

"Midge? It's Davida. The lady who gave you the dog?" Davida hesitated outside the shed, peering in the gap of the door.

"Oh! Hi, Davida! Is this your cat? My, he's a sweet little boy. He knew I was getting lonely in here."

"Midge! What are you doing out here all alone? It's freezing in here!" Davida pushed the door open. Whenever someone else was suffering, he r own emotions didn't matter. She was no longer scared. Midge might not be "all there" according to some people, but she was a sweet, kind woman with a childlike innocence and a good heart.

"I'm waiting for Preston to call me. See? He gave me this new phone."

"He did? What a nice Christmas present."

Midge nodded. "He loves me, you know. Some people say he's not a good brother, but I know he's a good brother. He came to visit me yesterday."

"That *is* nice! Can we talk about it inside? Look at you. You're all dressed for the party."

"I went to the party." Midge made a face. "It was too loud. I don't like parties. I stayed in my room most of the time."

"Your... old room? Your room in the manor?"

"Yes. When I came in, I saw Dr. Lori and she told me I didn't have to stay long, but it was nice of me to come."

"I'm so sorry I didn't see you come in. But... what are you doing out here? Oh, because it would be too noisy to hear the phone ring when Preston calls?" Davida patted Midge's hand, crouching to kneel next to her. Privately, she wondered if Preston would ever call his sister. It seemed mean to give her the phone and then not use it—and Preston's unkindness wasn't the main problem right now. "The party will be over soon. It's almost midnight. Who brought you to the party?" She knew Midge didn't drive.

"Oh, Briarwood Court sent a lot of us over together in the van with Father Ben and Mrs. Simmons. Briarwood Episcopal is very active with us. They have Wednesday Bible Study in the common room you know. They take us on little outings. They even paid for our tickets tonight if we couldn't afford them."

"That's lovely! I did see some of your neighbors, Midge. I'm sorry I didn't see you. I know it's loud, but please come back to the house. You'll get sick out here," Davida insisted, daring to reach for Midge's shoulder.

Midge shied away. "No. No, no. I'm waiting here."

A sinking feeling, one not related to the oddity of a kiddie playhouse in the midst of a deep, overgrown woods, came over her. "Why can't you wait for Preston to call inside, where it's warm?"

Midge bit her lower lip, the image of a worried girl in a much older woman's face.

"Is something wrong with Preston?" Davida nudged.

"No! No, he's just busy. He's very busy." Midge blinked rapidly and ran the sleeve of her thick mauve coat over her eyes, smearing her overabundance of powder blue eye shadow across her cheek.

"Midge? I can keep a secret. Tell me what's wrong. Oh! And I have a quiet, warm place where you can wait for your call."

Midge hesitated, then rose. "Just for a few minutes."

"Of course."

Davida backed away and opened the door, shivering as a fresh blast of cold air hit her legs. She cradled Sparkler in one arm, nuzzling the cat's soft head. "You were a good boy, indeed. I knew you were a people person." She moved the flashlight along the floor to light their path. To her surprise, Midge stopped at the door, and ran her withered, wrinkled fingers along the upper edge. Something dull and brass glinted before it disappeared into Midge's palm. Something small.

The size of a penny... or a padlock key.

Oh, no.

Preston must have got Midge in on his crusade to close down the shelter. He probably told her she could move back home. He probably played on her happy childhood memories. Davida cleared her throat as they picked their way along the twisting, overgrown path back to the driveway. "Midge. Is there something you've been missing?"

Midge let out a muffled sob. "H-how did you guess?"

"Well, honey, it's not hard to imagine someone missing their childhood home! Being back at Pembroke must have made you homesick, huh? Maybe you thought you could... you could *borrow* some money and buy the place back?" Davida suggested, rubbing soothing circles on the hunched shoulders beside her.

"Miss this place? Move back? Oh no. No, no. I couldn't leave Lily, Rosie, and Mary. And Father Ben and Mrs. Simmons! Briarwood Court is my home. I love it there. I have everything just the right size... almost like a big playhouse. I can take care of it all on my own and my friends check in on me. They never used to check in on me here."

Davida kept silent. She suspected the older woman didn't have friends when she lived as recluse at the rundown manor. But then—what was she missing? Her brother? She supposed it was possible, even if he seemed like a jerk.

"Why don't you tell me what you're missing, and what Preston is going to call you about?"

As they reached the blessed smoothness of the pavement, Davida flipped over her phone and texted Naveen.

Safe. At office.

"Preston hasn't come to see me since I sold the house. But I didn't expect him to. He never came to see me, not since Mommy and Daddy moved to Florida."

It was only by clenching her teeth that Davida managed to swallow down some incredibly rude names for Preston.

"My other brother lives faraway, but he calls me and he comes up at Christmas. Did you know he came up at Thanksgiving this year?"

Davida shook her head with a polite smile. "That must have been nice."

"It was! Oh, and he loved meeting Tiger. But Preston... Preston has no time for pets. Unneeded expenses, he always said. But when he heard Tiger was missing! Oh my. Oh my, Miss Maxwell, he sprang into action!"

"Tiger is missing? What? Since when? Thanksgiving?"

"What? Oh, no, dear. Tiger went missing the night before last. Preston came to see me, and I was so upset I could hardly enjoy his visit, even though he brought me a bottle of the perfume I used to wear when I was a girl and my favorite chocolates— mint cups. And the phone, of course."

"Midge, back to Tiger being missing. How did he get out? Did you search? No one called the shelter to ask if he'd been turned in."

"I don't know how it happened," Midge wailed as they walked into the warmth of the office. "Preston came. I ate some of the chocolates he brought me—I never could resist mint cups and they were in such a pretty box— and then I excused myself to take a nap as soon as he left. When I woke up, Tiger wasn't in my little bungalow. None of the girls had seen him. None of the staff knew where he was! Oh, we looked all over the common areas and everyone searched their rooms. I was so upset. I was going to call you, but then Preston called me on the new phone he gave me. When he heard what happened, he told me he would handle everything. He would hire a team of special private detectives who specialize in missing pets. And he did!"

"He did?" Davida put Sparkler down on the desk, knowing full well no cage was worthwhile. The kitten crept over to Midge as she sat on the edge of her chair, wringing her hands. The kitten nudged its head under one anxious palm, and Midge began to stroke it, her voice steadying as she did so.

"It was very kind of Preston. He said he would handle everything, even if it meant missing his New Year's Eve plans." Midge dropped her voice. "He said I had to come and pick up Mommy's envelope for him."

Davida stiffened at the word 'envelope.' "What envelope, Midge?"

"The one Woody took."

"Woody. Woodbine? The *mayor*?" Davida decided to sit. It was better for her brain, which was currently whizzing around in her head.

"Oh, Woody and Preston were always fighting when they were kids. Woody took an envelope Mommy gave Preston, but he was finally going to give it back. Preston was supposed to pick it up tonight, but he said he'd find Tiger for me instead."

"So you came to get the envelope since he was busy helping you?" An ugly scenario unfolded in Davida's head. She had no way of knowing if it was true or not.

Preston knows Midge will be above suspicion. He visits his sister out of the blue. He drugs her candy with a sedative. He pretends to leave, but really goes around the back, and then takes Tiger away. He calls a little later and tells Midge he'll find the dog if she'll cover for him. And since Midge trusts everyone...

"Preston told me he would put it in my old keepsake box. Why, there it is." Midge pointed to the ornately carved box on the desk. "This matched my bedroom set. My bedstead, my dresser, the wardrobe, my jewelry box, and this was my secret box. I kept chocolate in it."

"This is your box? But—But it was donated to us just yesterday for the fundraiser."

"Oh, I haven't had it in years. When Preston moved out, he took some of the furniture. He had my box, but he wouldn't give it back. I don't mind anymore. I just want my dog back!"

"I'm going to make *sure* you get Tiger back," Davida said. Her thumb flew across the screen.

Naveen: Any luck? It's almost midnight!
Me: Mayor, sheriff, office now.

"Do you know the dog detectives?" Midge's watery eyes lit up. "Preston said I'm not allowed to call him. If I do, it might scare off Tiger just as he's about to nab him."

"I don't know the dog detectives, but I have a good idea about where I can find Tiger... or someone who does. So tell me about this envelope from your mother."

"I don't know what's in it. I think it's money Preston was minding for me that Woody took. Although... I don't know about that. Preston was rather a naughty little boy. He took Woody's toys far more often than Woody ever took his!"

"How did you know what envelope to take? Did it have your mother's name on it? Or Preston's?"

"Oh no, Woody wouldn't want anyone to know he had something of Preston's for all these years. Preston told me just what Woody would do. He'd make a big splash about putting the envelope in the box, like it was some noble thing. That would be the signal. Then I should find a time to use my key and get it back."

"You had the key to the padlock? Well—what if I'd used a different one?" Davida clutched her head. Nikki had given her the box from Jilly Strache (supposedly a special gift from the antique store just for the gala!). It had a small but sturdy silver padlock with a single key attached.

"Well, I don't think *this* is my old lock. I had one with the knobs that spins. The combination was always my birthday," Midge whispered as if sharing a secret.

"But how did you have the key?"

"Preston said he'd leave it for me in the old playhouse. When I was done getting the envelope, I was supposed to put it back in the old hiding spot. We always kept the spare key to the house over the inside of the door in the playhouse. Sure enough, there it was. He must've stopped by and left it for me. But even if he hadn't, Preston would know that I can pick most locks. He used to lock me in my room sometimes when Mommy and Daddy went out for dinner. I always got out. It was our little game."

Davida didn't say anything. Preston Pembroke, aside from being absolute scum, wouldn't be careless enough to be seen on the premises on the night that a theft occurred. However, someone who had access to the lock box and the keys that came with the padlock HAD been there that night. Jilly Strache had dropped off the box to Nikki yesterday, and had dropped off her mother tonight. Her mother who owned the antique shop but had claimed never to have seen that particular box. Jilly Strache, who had some mysterious boyfriend who she met at the bank... where she worked in real estate. Jilly Strache, who used to work for Mayor Woodbine.

"It fits. It fits too neatly."

"The key?" Midge frowned.

"No..." Davida trailed off. This would be too easy—except for the fact that they couldn't prove any of it. Not a word. Nothing but guesswork and the half-clues Midge provided. No judge would ever consider a fully reliable witness.

"Midge, I think there was a different envelope you were supposed to get. It was dark, remember? You might not have been able to see well."

"It was dark. I threw the breakers to the downstairs room. The breaker box is in the closet just beside the kitchen, in case you didn't know."

"That'll come in handy. Midge, you're a font of information. Your information could help a lot of animals find good homes."

Midge looked away, face twisting with guilt. "Did Preston do something bad?"

"Maybe. I think we'll know more when you call him."

"I can't! I like animals, Davida, but I love Tiger. Tiger is my best friend. And... And I know I have to help you. I was a Tiger Scout growing up, you know." Midge held up three shaking fingers. "Tigers have three stripes, three, Courage, Kindness, and Hon-est-y!" she chanted.

"You have been very honest and brave. And you're very kind, too. You know, there is a simple way to see if there's really anything wrong. Just open the envelope."

"But I can't! Preston said he'd know if I did. He said if I broke my promise, he'd break his. I'll never see Tiger again!"

"Davida?"

"Miss Maxwell?"

Midge jumped as the mayor, the sheriff, and Naveen came in. She let out a little strangled cry and clutched Sparkler tight.

"Oh! Oh, perfect. Midge, just sit there and play with Sparkler. Um, here. He loves to chase pens across my desk." Davida dumped out her pencil cup and the kitten bounded across the desk, paws outstretched in mid-pounce. Davida hustled the three bewildered men out of the office and into the now empty kennel.

"Miss Maxwell, what's going on?"

"Mayor Woodbine, I'm going to need you to trust me and not ask a lot of questions."

"Well, I'm game for anything. It's been quite a party!" Mayor Woodbine chuckled. "What can I do?"

Davida pulled a blank business envelope, a sticky note, and pen from her coat pocket, smirking at the shocked looks on their faces. "I need you to jot a little note to Preston Pembroke."

CHAPTER EIGHT

"Miss Pembroke! So nice to see you out and about. I'm sorry about that little mix-up. Here's the envelope I have for your dear brother. Do tell him I'm sorry about hanging on to it for so long." Mayor Woodbine presented Midge with an envelope in his outstretched hand.

Midge stopped batting an eraser for Sparkler to chase. "Wh-what? You have it?"

"I do indeed! I wouldn't be so careless as to put a personal note for Preston in the box with all the donations. May we trade?" Mayor Woodbine bowed over Midge's hand with a charming smile.

"I thought it was a silly way to collect a note. That Preston! He always liked to play pranks on me." Midge reached inside her coat and slid a hand into the capacious folds of her beaded purple dress. "It's in here someplace."

Mayor Woodbine took the envelope with a pained smile as it finally reappeared from somewhere in the midst of Midge's dress. He passed it to Davida as quickly as possible.

Davida sagged in relief and found herself supported by Naveen. "Not a disaster after all," he murmured into her hair.

"Not yet. Um. Sheriff, you might have to help Midge. You see, Preston hired a bunch of special dog detectives to find Tiger. Tiger went missing yesterday, just after Midge and Preston had a snack together."

"Yes, I got so sleepy. I went to lay down. When I woke up, it was hours later and Tiger was missing. But Preston is handling it."

"I'll just bet he handled it." The sheriff in black exchanged a dark look with Davida. "Why don't you and I wait here for him to call you and give you an update. Don't tell him I'm here. Just say you've got the envelope from the mayor and you want to pick up your dog. If it's been found, of course. Tell you what, I'll give you a lift to get Tiger."

"If he isn't waiting for you safely at home." Naveen shook his head, hands clenched.

He catches on quick, Davida thought to herself. "If we run, we can make it to the ballroom by midnight! Mr. Mayor?"

"After you, dear host and hostess!"

Davida and Naveen ran ahead of the older man. At some point, tripping and sliding in her heels, she'd clutched his arm for support, and now they raced along, hand in hand.

"You have to fill me in!" he panted as they skidded to a stop on the patio.

"We have to have a lot of conversations."

"I'm looking forward to them. I have a ton of questions."

"I have just one. Where are the dogs?"

Davida got her answer as they entered the ballroom.

Three pitbull mixes were lying next to Luke and his band mates.

Three more were getting belly rubs and being hand fed charcuterie scraps by the buffet table.

An elderly senior dog with thick cataracts was snoring softly with his head in the lap of Mrs. Woodbine.

Others were scattered around the room, clearly the life of the party.

"Dang. I could have saved on champagne and just let the dogs come to the party," Davida marveled.

"That was my idea."

"Yeah, well... maybe that's why we make a good team."

"It's countdown time!" Luke broke off the jazzy patter he was playing and held the mic up by the cord. "Ready for the mic drop? Ten! Nine!"

"Get up there," Naveen propelled her through the crowd.

"I will in a few seconds." Davida looked around, realizing that she was still holding Naveen's hand. "You know all of this was risk? Taking all of my savings for the down payment, leaving law school... Trying to solve the mystery of the missing check before anyone found out..."

"Your risks pay off, it seems."

"Yeah."

"Four! Three!"

"I'm going to take another one. Want to take it with me?" Davida blurted.

Naveen nodded. "I know a good horse to bet on when I see it."

"I'll take that as a compliment."

"One! Happy New Year!"

The room erupted with cheering and barking. Davida pressed her lips to Naveen's, shocked when he kissed her back, dipping her low over his arm in a dizzying sweep.

When he pulled her upright, she was out of breath. "You don't do anything halfway, huh?"

"Nope. Now go. Get up there."

"You, too! I couldn't have done this without you."

As Davida marched to the microphone on Naveen's arm, the cheering intensified. "Thank you all! Thank you so much! Because of all your hard work and generosity, we've raised over forty thousand dollars!"

"And I'm here to make it eighty!" Mayor Woodbine stepped up to join them.

"And a dog!" Mrs. Woodbine called out.

"What?" Mayor Woodbine looked flabbergasted, which made the crowd hoot with laughter. Being a consummate politician and a son of Briarwood through and through, he knew enough to laugh along. "All right, all right. Eighty thousand and a dog! From the looks of it, it seems I'm not the only one who intends to leave the party with a new friend."

"Adoption forms are at the office, which opens at nine. I'll even make an exception and do business on a holiday!" Davida waved to a few families who had clearly gotten attached to the mutts they'd partied with.

"Who gets the kitten?" a voice called.

"The kitten?" Davida looked around. She'd left Sparkler in the office with Midge and the sheriff.

"That kitten!" The man pointed to the tables that were set up as a makeshift bar.

Davida gasped as she found the target of the gentleman's inquiries. Sparkler was leaning over a giant punchbowl, trying to bat a circle of lemon floating in a sea of pink. "Oh, Sparkler, no!"

Splash! "Mrow!" Sparkler jumped off and streaked through the room, wet and scraggly looking with a bit of lemon stuck on his tail. He made a beeline for Davida and leapt into her arms.

Naveen took the microphone. "The lady gets the kitten."

"MIDGE? DO YOU HAVE it?" Preston Pembroke's voice was muffled.

"I have it. What did the detective say?"

"Wait a minute, Midge. Tell me about the party. Any interesting events? Any... police activity?"

"The sheriff came to Miss Maxwell's office." Midge narrowed her eyes in confusion. "Why?"

"Just curious. That's not important. You go home and you'll have a wonderful surprise. A friend of mine, Jilly, is dropping off Tiger."

"Oh, Pres! You found him!"

"Yep, yep. He's just fine. A little confused, but fine. As for that envelope, you give it to Jilly, you hear?"

"Okay, Preston, I will. I'll come home right now!"

"I guess the party's over, huh?" Preston chuckled in satisfaction.

Midge looked out the window. People were making their way to the parking area. "Yep. It's all over."

"Perfect. See you soon. Well, not me personally. I'll be out of town for a few weeks until I sign a real estate deal. But after that, I'll be around a lot more."

"That'll be great, Preston. Maybe this time Elizabeth can come with you?"

"Ah. Maybe not. But you might see Jilly with me. She's... she's been helping me at the bank. Happy New Year, sis. You finally did something right."

Midge looked at the sheriff as the call disconnected. "How do I hang up?" she asked.

The sheriff gently turned off his own phone, which had recorded the conversation. "It's over already, sweetie. Come on. I'll take you home to that pup of yours."

EPILOGUE

"I have a migraine."

"I have coffee."

"I think I love you."

"Well, I'm extremely lovable."

Davida opened her door on New Year's Day. It was eight AM. She'd had about five hours of sleep. It was hard getting used to a cat sharing her pillow.

Naveen, neighbor and possibly new boyfriend, appeared at her door with a cup of coffee, dressed in jeans and a cable knit sweater.

"Still handsome. It wasn't my party goggles," she swiped a kiss across his cheek and took the coffee eagerly.

"I didn't see you have more than one glass of champagne. Why the headache?"

"Stress. Not a lot of sleep. I can't believe I let all those people go home with dogs. That's not really shelter protocol."

"Everyone was a local. Luke's drummer, that nurse from the clinic, Father Ben, the mayor and his wife... They're all good people."

"Hmm. You changed your tune."

"Someone taught me a new song."

"Yet you still need the last word," Davida sighed, draining her mug.

"I bet we're on the local news. That was quite a party." Naveen sauntered to the living room and clicked his tongue. Sparkler immediately raced over and leapt onto his lap.

Davida watched him fondle the cat's ears as it snuggled into his sweater. I could get used to this. She joined them on the couch and clicked on the set. "We just have a few minutes. I have people coming in to do adoption paperwork, remember?"

"Yes, I remembered, hence bringing you coffee. And I thought I'd come with you. I have to set up my office. And you need someone to help you keep an eye on this little menace."

"Speaking of menace..." Davida froze as Preston Pembroke's face appeared on the screen.

"Briarwood native and current frozen food mogul Preston Pembroke and his mistress were arrested as the sun rose on a new year. I'm sure it wasn't the bright future they'd been planning," June Fairchild, the local news anchor explained and shook her head.

"Wonder what charge they got them on," Naveen leaned forward eagerly.

"Poor Andrea. I hope Jilly gets off lightly. She was only doing what Preston told her to do. It sounds like she was entranced by a wealthy older man."

"Still. She went along with it."

"Sad news, June. What was the crime?" Rick Randall, the meteorologist asked.

"You'll never believe this, Rick. Both of them were arrested with conspiracy to commit dog-napping. Fortunately, the victim, a three-year-old terrier-mix was returned safely to his owner. We'll have further updates as the case unfolds."

"Dog-napping. Yep. I knew it. I'm in a hick town, if that's the big news." Naveen leaned back on the couch with a wide stretch.

Davida turned off the television. "You'll notice they didn't mention theft, fraud, drugging, misrepresentation—"

Naveen rose and caught her hands as they gestured in midair. "There's a lot more under the surface in these places."

"In every place." Her annoyance melted away when he was this close, holding her hands, gazing into her eyes. "You like it here, right?"

"I don't want to be anywhere else. I don't want to move an inch. Well... maybe just a couple of inches." He bent his head, letting his lips come to a fraction away from hers.

"Good." Davida smiled as she kissed him.

For once, she got the last word.

Thank you for reading. If you enjoyed this book, look for news of my other *Holiday Pet Sleuth Mystery* Series releases on my website or socials linked below!

Read on for a sneak peak of *Framed by the Fireworks*, an M. Culler *Holiday Pet Sleuth* Mystery.

You can find all of the Holiday Pet Sleuth Mysteries HERE[1].

Do you love romance and historical mysteries, too?

Read on for a sneak peek of *The Undertaker's Daughter* by M. Culler, releasing 1/23/23 from The Wild Rose Press.

---

1.   https://www.amazon.com/dp/

B0B9SFP5KW?binding=kindle_edition&ref=dbs_dp_rwt_sb_pc_tukn

The Undertaker's Daughter

H arkness and Sons stood apart from any other building in the crowded corner of its East London dwelling place. It was as if fate had decided to protect the surrounding citizens from rubbing shoulders with death's earthly representatives.

Oh, it was all too true that death and the East End were no strangers. Her squalid yards and overflowing doss houses meant nightly contributions to the body merchants who would take the poor and unfortunate inhabitants to their final destination, not one of the overflowing and foul city churchyards, but to large baskets outside of hospitals and anatomy clinics where porters would collect them in the morning. Aspiring surgeons would spend days dissecting and breaking down a body, faces wrapped in camphor-soaked cloths to block the stench. When flesh was properly separated from bone, everything was sewn up in sturdy cotton sheets and buried in a giant pit on the far reaches of the hospital grounds.

Not so for the clients of Harkness and Sons. Reginald Harkness, Proprietor, Undertaker, and Director of Funeral Services, had a state-of-the-art facility for the dearly departed. No more calling for the undertaker, the coffin-maker, the shroud-maker, the feather-wavers, and the funeral carriage as separate entities. Harkness and Sons would supply all the services required for one fee, a one-stop shopping experience for the recently bereaved.

Unfortunately, Mr. Reginald Harkness, a distinguished man with an appropriately sympathetic face, was also a one-man operation. He was the only remaining son of Harkness and Sons, a reputable firm of undertakers since His Majesty George III's time. Fathers and sons had kept the business going, but now it seemed that its doors would be shuttered when Mr. Harkness joined his clientele.

No daughter of his would run the family business—even if she seemed oddly keen to do so.

"CHARLOTTE! CHARLOTTE?" Reginald poked his head into the kitchen. Clean. No smells of cooking. He sighed. "Charlotte, are you—" The brassy pealing of the bell from the back garden made Reginald abandon the search for his daughter.

Most women, certainly women with a clever mind like Charlotte's, should have been pursuing studies suitable to her sex, perhaps art, music, or sewing. The business made a good income, enough to help the girl set up her own shop. She could find employment as a seamstress or perhaps a milliner? A florist would have been ideal as he would have loved to supply flowers for the funeral carriages as well.

He had no illusions that Charlotte, even though she was radiantly beautiful to his proud paternal eyes, would easily find a husband. Who would come to pay her court here, with coffins in the small showroom that had once been his late wife's parlor and open-sided carriages coming to the back gate instead of lovesick boys with bouquets?

Speaking of carriages, Mr. Bartlesby was just coming to collect the coffin and shroud for the late Mr. Samuels. "Charlotte."

"Yes, Father?" A sweet face with wide blue eyes and curling golden hair arranged in a mass of pins atop her head poked around the door from the "laying-out" room.

Mr. Harkness jumped. "What are you doing in there?"

"Keeping Mrs. Perkins company until the vicar comes to collect her this afternoon."

"Charlotte, I've told you—"

"I know the spirit has gone on, Father, but imagine what it must've been like, to live ever so long and then to be taken ill so quickly and that mean landlady unwilling to leave her lie until the gravediggers could prepare a space in the churchyard. The cheek."

Her father rolled his eyes heavenward. "Charlotte, a lady mustn't say things like that."

An impish grin crossed her face. "At least I didn't say blo—"

"Dear me. Listen, Mr. Bartlesby is here, and I must go collect the late Mr. Samuels. The vicar won't come until after tea. If he's early, give him a cup of tea and a biscuit—"

"We're out of biscuits."

"Then be useful and bake some biscuits, finish sewing those shrouds I've been reminding you about for a week, and take some money to the flower stalls and get the usual." He swiftly kissed her cheek, jamming his black silk top hat on his head. "You forgot to steam the brim." One side of the brim had lost some of its elegant curl.

"Yes, Father, I will." Charlotte ducked her head to kiss his cheek in return, mindful not to knock the hat askew.

"Thank you. And Charlotte?"

"Yes?"

"For heaven's sake, don't let the vicar catch you 'chatting' to the dearly departed."

As her father hurried away, Charlotte sighed. "It's not my fault. It's not like I start the conversations. I'm simply too polite to ignore them."

CHARLOTTE ROLLED OUT shortbread biscuits. They were easy to make and her father's favorite. She was debating whether to run to the flower stalls in the market or put the leg of mutton in for supper.

"When Mr. Perkins worked for Smithfield, we had such lovely chops and all the tripe you could ask for, calves' feet, too. But cruel to the beasts, they were."

Charlotte sighed. Mrs. Perkins was a very chatty soul—literally. "Isn't he waiting for you?"

"Oh, I imagine so, dear, but you were so kind to come and settle me down when I found m'self all discombobulated, neither being here or there, you might say. A nice light hand with the dough you've got. Make someone a good wife."

"Thank you." It was no point in arguing with the gregarious and nebulous voice inside her head. She was not the marrying kind. She was the kind that was one step away from a permanent spot in an asylum, or at least the Yorkshire Dales.

The Yorkshire Dales were where her mother's sister, her aunt Kate, lived with her strapping farmer husband and their three enormous sons. To her father's way of thinking, the place radiated wholesomeness, clean air, sound bodies, and sound minds. It was the latter he believed Charlotte was lacking.

"I'm not mad, you know," Charlotte muttered.

"Are you talking to yourself? Sign of being touched in the head," Mrs. Perkins tutted.

"I'm not touched. You're here, aren't you?"

"I seem to be. S'pose it's because I haven't been properly buried. Do you think that's why?"

She slid the biscuits into the black-leaded oven and shut the door with a bang. Charlotte wished she could answer in the affirmative, but it hadn't been the case. Her mother had died years ago now, and she still heard her voice sometimes, felt her presence like a fleeting shaft of sun when passing by a window on a bright day. Her governess, whom she'd called Auntie Molly, had died four years ago and never made a peep or an appearance.

"I think that's why," Mrs. Perkins continued. "Makes sense, don't it? That must be why there's ghosts at places where wars were fought, haunting the battlefields. Some like as never got buried the proper way."

"Then why do they think the Tower is haunted? The executed were buried." Charlotte was beginning to feel cross. Most of the spirits who decided to speak to her needed a simple nudge, a little kind explanation. You've passed away. Your soul must go on. Yes, the body is in good hands, my father is the best in the business. But some... She fetched her hat and shawl with a sigh. "I'm going to go out as soon as the biscuits are baked."

"What? And waste all that good fire you've got going? Mutton ought to be roasted long and slow, dearie."

"I'll build another fire up." Impatience crept over Charlotte.

"Must be nice for them's that can."

Charlotte turned toward the direction of the nebulous presence, feeling its location rather than being able to see the owner of the scolding matronly voice. Mrs. Perkins' tone held quiet disapproval.

Charlotte told herself that was the bulk of her troubles.

I can't please anyone, alive or dead.

She was quite relieved to leave the house and hurry through the damp, chill air to the flower stalls. Mrs. Perkins hadn't realized that she could follow her and that was a bit of a relief.

"HELLO, MISS HARKNESS." Bob doffed his flat, rather stained cap.

"Hello, Miss Harkness, how's your father keeping?" His wife shuffled forward, a smile on her round, ruddy face.

"Hello, Bob. Hello, Mary. He's busy today. What have you got?"

"Mums and daisies, mainly, miss. It's the season, miss, losing the summer flowers."

"I imagine. Winter is a busy season for us, too. Consumption. So much worse in winter." Charlotte made conversation with Bob and his wife, loading her basket with flowers, buying them out, and feeling a bit guilty about it.

"You could do them fake flowers like they have on hats?" Mary suggested.

"I might have to, but they cost a lot more." Charlotte, for all the flaws her father gently assured her she possessed, was very clever with money.

"Well, you'll charge it back to the customers, won't you?"

"I suppose we'd have to. Although I was thinking we could do pine and holly. That would look nice, surely?"

"I suppose it would, miss."

Charlotte looked at the slate by the wooden cart filled with baskets and surrounded with barrels, now fairly empty. She counted out the coins quickly and passed them to Bob, who made notes in a scrawl that must've meant something to him, though it was indecipherable to her.

"And an apple for you and one for your father," Mary insisted, pressing them on top of the flowers.

"That's very kind, thank you."

"You could get a few more and make up a nice apple tart for your father," Bob hinted.

"Bob," Mary scolded. "Pushy devil."

Charlotte smiled and shook her head. "I've made his favorite shortbreads and I have to get on. The vicar will be coming after tea. I need to get the mutton in the oven."

"Ahh, pretty girl, she cooks, and she's good with figures. Mark my words, Miss Charlotte, you'll be needing your wedding flowers by the summer."

Charlotte laughed and waved. Bob and Mary were a devoted little couple, both with plump faces and weather-beaten hands, both missing a few teeth, and wearing the same worn brown coats no matter the weather. While Charlotte and her father lived near Tower Field, in a more prosperous area, she had gathered that Mary and Bob lived farther afield from the market, a long way down the Whitechapel High Street, right before St. Clementia's. St. Clementia's was a tiny, unadorned church that was the last bastion of respectability before squalor, opium dens, and houses of low character took over beyond the main road. The deeper you went, the worse it got. When Mary had suffered a bad fall in January, Charlotte had been all for taking them a meat pie. Her father had nearly needed to be outfitted for a coffin of his own.

A lady must never, ever, ever venture past St. Clementia's at night, unescorted, or at all, he had thundered, idly shredding January's Undertaker's Gazette in his distress.

Why he'd bothered with mentioning night or unaccompanied when he was going to add "at all" was beyond her. He didn't much care for Charlotte pointing that out, either.

"Mind your reticule and basket, Miss Charlotte." Mary always reminded her of this when she turned to leave, her voice a wary whisper, eyes roving through the crowded market. Today was no exception. "Are you heading straight home?"

"I'll be careful, Mary, and yes." Charlotte's smile was strained. Heaven only knew what girls ten years her junior were doing on London streets, selling flowers, fish, fruits, or something else, walking alone day or night, living alone, like old Mrs. Perkins. To say nothing of the boys!

But she was a "lady" of good family and respectable status, hovering around the upper bit of middle-class, she supposed. As she hurried home, keeping her eyes properly averted, she couldn't help but wonder. Was it for her protection as a person or the protection of her reputation that she mustn't venture too far from the main streets in the better parts of the city?

"Both, little bird," her mother's voice seemed to breathe against her ear.

"OHHH. OH, YOU MUSTN'T say such wicked things." Lavinia Everly giggled and fluttered dark black lashes that framed laughing brown eyes.

"But I must when you encourage me so." Her companion bent his head, his dark, curling locks combed in the latest rakish style. They tumbled forward, hiding his mischievous eyes. His lips flicked the soft skin of her ear and watched her shiver. Something in him shuddered, too. Disgust. Desire.

It was a constant struggle for supremacy.

Just like her, just like a woman. She shied away from his touch on her neck, his hand pulling her too intimately close, and yet if he should treat her with cold reserve, she was cloying and clinging, a leech upon his elbow.

Yes, women were all the same, vines choking the flowers, pretending to be so helpless when really they were the devils who would ensnare unsuspecting men. Like Lavinia did now, shuddering from his touch like a shrinking violet, but urging him with squeezes on his arm as the cab rambled over the cobbles.

A wave of fog rolled in, carrying a sepulchral stench and a metallic taste on the tongue. Outside, the driver coughed violently, startling Lavinia into speech.

"Why, where are we?" She craned her neck and drew back with a gasp. "Oh. Oh my. This is the place you wished to bring me?"

"You wouldn't be allowed in my rooms, and your mother won't have me 'round, now that she knows my prospects are bleak," he informed her bitterly. Anger flared again. She wanted to meet but can't be seen with me in public. What did she expect me to do?

"Why, you'll keep us fine. Mother's got money; I'm sure Father left us plenty," Lavinia said complacently.

Another dead father. His own had passed. Hardly been cold before his mother married again, a florid-faced man with a title, a baronet with a decent estate. She promptly bore him a son to pass the title on to as well. This ensured that he, the unwanted stepson, would have nothing but his late father's legacy, whatever was left that his mother hadn't spent in catching her second husband's eye.

With an angry rap, he bade the driver stop and handed Lavinia down from the carriage with a whirl of skirts and nervous giggles.

"Can't we go to your mother's home? Oh, no, I suppose it is too far for a night's journey. But I must be back soon. Mother doesn't know I've left, you know."

"No?" The blackness behind his eyes suddenly ticked up a notch.

"I told her I'd gone to bed with a headache. She found your last letter to me, and she and I had such a row."

"Thank heavens I didn't sign it."

"Oh, but you did." Lavinia sighed dreamily. "Not with your true name, but still. Love, Jack. How deliciously scandalous it is, our clandestine meetings, secretly posting letters, using an assumed name lest Mama intercept them..."

He said nothing, taking her arm and looking above the doors for a house that had a large lantern swinging from an iron hook. Any one would do.

"Is this where you stay when you come to the city?" Lavinia's voice was a tiny squeak.

"Fourpence gets you in," he said shortly, steering past leering drunkards and beggars. He pushed her roughly through the pile of refuse and filth outside the battered doorway. She let out a little squeak and all but fell into the dark hall.

A beggar's hand grabbed his pocket. Darting a glance at his floundering companion, he made a quick decision. A violent punch sent the man's head cracking into the exterior wall with a sickening crushing sound. Was it the wood or his skull?

"No matter," he muttered.

"Want a room?"

Lavinia shrieked as if someone had stabbed her with a hatpin. He rolled his eyes and dropped money into the outstretched palm of a very dirty and wizened old crone, her face barely visible over layers of lice-ridden blankets.

"All the way in the back. On the right. Out in the morn by ten or pays again!"

"Yes." He curtly nodded and steered Lavinia ahead of him.

The houses of Registered Common Lodging were usually all the same, a den for thieves and whores, or worse. They didn't care for the cleanliness if they were saved from a night in jail or a night freezing to death in the elements. The government officers who were supposed to be stamping out the filth, disease, and crime of the London slums rarely came to inspect the worst premises. If they did, they could usually be bought off for a song.

As he opened the door, he saw a stripped bed, a chamber pot that was mercifully empty, and a three-legged stool.

"Oh! Oh, we can't stay here," Lavinia hissed, her voice quaking with fear. "I saw a mouse."

"You'll see a rat in a minute." He laughed. "Come now, you wanted to be alone with me. Implored me so sweetly in your letter. How did you post that?"

"Mama has not been well. The doctor came round last week, and I sent it with Sadie, the maid."

"She didn't think it was odd?"

"Sadie can't read. She wouldn't think it odd if she could; the poor thing can barely think at all!" She laughed as if she'd said something very clever.

"Hm. But she can clean and cook and dress her lady in finery?" He kissed her gloved hand.

Lavinia hesitated, letting his lips linger as her eyes closed. He knew Lavinia was aware of his eyes on her. She lit up under his attention. She took off her hat, carefully setting it on the stool with a swish of her hips, letting her long ebony hair fall free. "What brains does one need for cooking and cleaning?" she simpered.

"Let's see your talents then."

"You've heard me sing and play the pianoforte."

"Very lovely it was, too. But what else have you got to offer a man?" *What else, but what you think I want, a chance to rut inside you like some filthy beast...*

Maybe you're right, Lavinia. We'll see.

"We... mustn't."

"Mustn't do what?" he led, stealing a kiss from her paling lips.

"I want to go home!" Lavinia pushed him off with a pout.

"Fine. Go home. There's the door."

"I can't—I can't go alone."

"Then stay."

"Take me home right now."

Look at her, giving orders, so haughty, her dainty nose in the air when she's not looking down at you, that is. Worst kind of woman. The blackness raged. It fell. Let her escape. Escape yourself.

"As you wish." He retrieved her hat and held it out to her with a flourish.

"Wait." Lavinia bit her lip, nervously twisting the ornate piece of silk and ribbon he presented to her. "I... I know you wouldn't do anything wrong. It's only that meeting in a place like this seems so sinful!"

He held his tongue for a moment, then smiled. "Deceiving your mother isn't?"

"Don't talk me round in circles, you confuse me so," she said peevishly.

"Temper, temper." He leaned as near as he had in the coach, his arm stealing around her waist.

"Ohhh." Her eyes melted as they looked up at him. One moment so innocent, the next saucy. "Kiss it better?"

His lips met hers, and the shudders took him over as he gripped her arms hard, fingers grasping hard enough to bruise.

Maybe he'd be satisfied to hurt her just a little.

"CHARLOTTE?"

"Yes? One moment, Father." She concentrated hard on her sewing. That was the trouble with white shrouds. One drop of blood and the whole thing was spoiled. She had very little patience for hand-sewing and would have preferred to use their recently acquired sewing machine if this last bit mustn't be ruched up to cover the head. Charlotte was glad that for all her father's prudence with finances, he didn't make her sew her own dresses but always gave her a generous allowance for clothing and linens. "There. That's seven done. Do you think I need to do more?"

Her father scratched his chin. "Well. I talked to the vicar yesterday after he came to collect Mrs. Perkins. The members of the parish ladies' guild are raising funds for the elderly and infirm to help them eke out the winter. Still, anyone who doesn't survive it..."

Charlotte's eyes lit up. "Oh, Father! A sort of contract?"

"I'm pleased with the idea myself. But hearing my bright-eyed, pink-cheeked daughter say such things gives me pause. Charlotte, a lady ought not to—"

Charlotte turned the topic back to business, a skill she had mastered. "A lady ought to support her father in his endeavors. After all, a father's fortunes are his daughter's favors, is that not so?"

He sighed. "Indeed, and now that Kensley Green has opened up outside the city for burials, I've made arrangements with Mr. Pottsgrove, the property manager. He'll be sending referrals our way."

In spite of her father's reservations, Charlotte watched a smile spread across his face as he discussed his plans with her. Charlotte rushed from her sewing and hugged him, patting his hand eagerly. It was the sort of thing her mother would have done when he set up to improve the place, offering more services under one roof. "Mother would be so proud of you."

His smile vanished. "Charlotte, leave the sewing for now. Another seven would be welcome, just in case. I heard rumors that the pump on Bethnal Circle has been contaminated with the fever, and you know what that means."

She nodded gravely. "If the city won't see to it soon, we'll be dealing with that as well as the consumption and cold-related deaths this winter."

He nodded in return, the gravity on his face taking a different direction. "A girl shouldn't know so much about death."

"Oh, Father. Not this again."

"No, I'm serious. You're twenty-four, and you're very clever. You could turn your hand to so many things. Now, I know you want to help the family business. What about if we hire a storefront in the High Street? A flower shop. Mr. Mungabee is getting older and will want to retire soon. Those two in the market you're so fond of, Rob and Maudie—"

"Bob and Mary," she corrected automatically.

"They could help you with supply. We need the flowers, after all. You'd be helping provide those two some security. They're getting on in years," he led.

Charlotte's lips thinned. Yes, indeed, her father was a brilliant man. He knew just how to make her consider it, even for a moment.

The moment passed. "I prefer to help you on the premises. There's a lot to do that you would have to hire help for if you didn't have me. I'm a good savings, Father."

"No one could deny it."

She knew he couldn't deny it, which is why this discussion, which had happened every few months for the last four years, never arrived at a successful conclusion.

"You'd have to buy shrouds and hire an assistant to greet the funeral carriages and coffin-makers when you're out."

Her father made a noncommittal noise. "True."

Charlotte added to the list silently. She had a calm and cheerful demeanor. She smiled comfortingly and never seemed to feel squeamish. Perhaps that was the problem. If she'd ever been truly afraid or ill around the bodies that rarely ended up staying on the premises for more than a few hours, perhaps she wouldn't be so content to stay here, and she would be receptive to her father's attempts to get her away from Harkness and Sons, away from death.

"Charlotte. You're a great help to me. But it isn't fair to you to spend all of your time here, among the dead and the funeral furnishings."

"Why?"

"What?"

"Why isn't it fair? There's a sort of grace and dignity among those who've passed. They have lived their lives, good or evil, and they're finished. Only the Almighty has to deal with them now. Nothing they can do will change—"

"Nothing they can do? They're dead. There's nothing they do. Full stop."

She flushed. Her father's eyes narrowed suspiciously. Heat rose to her face, leaving her fingers cold. She hated lying to him. Lying was a sin. But being locked away when she wasn't insane would be a sin, too, wouldn't it?

"Are you hearing things again?" he whispered.

"I hear you plainly, Father."

"That's not what I mean. You said you were keeping Mrs. Perkins company. Oh, dear Lord, Charlotte, were you 'hearing' her, not simply being your incorrigible self?"

"Lots of people carry on conversations with what's around them, Father." This was not technically a lie. "I cannot tell you how often Auntie Molly used to argue with the oven. I hear you muttering insults at your waistcoat at least once a week, but it's not at fault when you find it snug." She abruptly got up. "Speaking of snug, Mary and Bob sent us two apples. Shall I bake them with cloves or try to make a small tart, just for the two of us?"

He followed her into the kitchen. "It's not madness to mutter an odd word or two to an uncooperative button or an oven that takes too long to get hot. It's madness if you think the oven is talking back."

"I've never heard a peep out of the oven. Now, I think I'll try that tart after all. We have just a bit of lard left."

Someone rapped on the front door. Her father's shoulders sagged. Charlotte knew that her father wanted to press her further, but he was clever enough to know there was no need. Her evasiveness would be enough to tell him his suspicions were correct.

REGINALD TRUDGED TOWARD the door, heart heavy.

His poor, dutiful daughter was deluded.

Or perhaps it was some strange female malady, hysteria from spending too much time alone. It wasn't his fault that she had no siblings. If Prudence hadn't passed... "Oh, Pru. I wish you'd help her get over this," he sighed to himself as he hurried to open the door and deal with yet another unexpected client.

As he listened patiently to a suddenly bereaved widow, he realized that his business was surely the most predictable and the most uncertain of all. Death visited everyone. It was capricious about how, when, and why. It was simply too much for a woman, especially a woman like Charlotte, with her wit and waspish tongue. Throw in her penchant for hearing voices from beyond the grave? He blamed himself.

Oh, Prudence, what did I do wrong? Should I have sent her away? I couldn't have borne it.

But I must now.

CHARLOTTE BROUGHT TWO cups of tea and two biscuits to her father and his guest, a working-class woman judging by her dress and shoes. Her father was providing price options in his gentlemanly way. She knew with almost total certainty that the woman would pick the two-pound funeral. It was probably all she could afford.

"I want my Ned to have the very best. I want the mutes. Feather-wavers." She had a defiant set to her chin as if daring Mr. Harkness to argue with her. "An open-sided carriage with flowers, lots of 'em, white ones."

"Erm. Yes. That will of course run into some money. The mutes are tuppence each. The open-sided carriage is of course part of our services. White flowers, now... Hm. Charlotte?"

"Daisies and yellow mums. Would your Ned have liked that?"

The woman looked at her with grateful, red-rimmed eyes. "Bless you, miss, I think he would. He said yellow was a cheery color."

"I'll make up a nice long strand to ring both sides of the coffin. Then a nice spray on top. Understated, but very elegant. Too showy might make Ned feel a little bit of a prig, don't you think?"

Another nod, another grateful glance. "That might be so. Yes, I'm sure that's so."

"He wouldn't want you to go all out on his last expenses, not out of proportion." Charlotte smoothed her skirts and sat down beside her. "Mrs.—?"

"Bailey."

"Mrs. Bailey, Ned would worry himself sick if he knew you were spending all of your savings on the funeral. What about the rent and everything to follow?"

"I'm going to live with my married daughter in Bolton. But you've a point. There's the fares to consider and the last month paying, not to mention the doctor's bill, not that he did any good, mind you." She dabbed at her eyes with a crumpled bit of cotton edged in tattered lace.

"The two-pound funeral will be quite a nice showing and with the mutes and feather-wavers that will bring it to two pounds and sixpence," Mr. Harkness jumped in. "Have you fixed the time for the services?"

Charlotte unobtrusively shrank away, back to the kitchen where she'd start weaving the daisies and mums into long strings, white thread and green stems. She could hear her father making arrangements about picking up the body the morning of the services. Fortunately, Mr. Bartlesby, their coach driver, always helped her father carry in the coffins and carry them out if there were no strong relatives of the deceased.

He really ought to have a son. Or even a son-in-law, I suppose. Although that would mean finding a man who was both interested in undertaking and in her.

"That may be nearly impossible," she lamented to the basket of daisies on the table.

WHEN MRS. BAILEY LEFT, Mr. Harkness found Charlotte diligently weaving flowers by lamplight. "Dear, you should go to bed. You could work on that tomorrow."

"Just let me finish this last bunch, Father."

"They do look lovely. You see, you have such a talent for it! You—erm—you could do very well with a flower shop of your own. You know we're much respected in the trade. You needn't work exclusively for our family, there would be dozens in the area who would want your services. Nor would it be confined to funerals. Weddings, Charlotte. Husbands celebrating birthdays. Young men paying calls. One might even decide to stop in to catch sight of something much more lovely than the bouquets." He rested a fond hand on the mass of falling curls.

Charlotte looked up at him with a smile. "That's a fine idea, Father. I'm not sure I'd enjoy that, though. I would like to stay on here, stay with you. You know... it's not that women don't already assist, Father. Usually, a local woman has already laid out the body when you arrive. It's rarely a man."

"I don't think they're affected by it in the same manner." His genial smile turned sad. "What about studies? You can read and write better than half the lads I went to school with. You're far better in maths. There's talk of some new ladies' college in Cheltenham. You're only twenty-four. That's not too late to attend, I'm sure."

"And what would I do when I've completed my studies? They won't let a woman study medicine. They surely won't let me study embalming—though heaven knows I could do it better than half the undertakers today."

"Charlotte!"

But she warmed to the subject, abandoning her flowers and pacing the kitchen. "Would you have me enter domestic service, become a ladies' maid or a housekeeper? I've dressed myself and managed this house nicely since Auntie Molly passed. I suppose I could be a governess to some other little girls who won't get to choose a career, either!"

"Career? My darling girl, your career is written in the Bible, to be a helpmeet! A wife and mother."

"Or a judge like Deborah, or a tentmaker like Priscilla, or a seller of purple like Lydia?"

"Well... well! Sell cloth if you like. Make dresses. Whatever you wish." Mr. Harkness enthused. "Better to make dresses rather than... Erm."

"Commune with the dead?" Charlotte supplied.

"Well. Yes."

"I wish you to change the shingle over our doorpost, Father. Harkness and Daughter."

Her father's relief departed abruptly. Cold calm replaced it. "No."

"You said whatever I wish. I wish to stay with you and help you!"

"No, I said."

"Mother helped you."

"A fat lot of good she did, dying on us and turning you funny, these visions and voices and—" A look of horror bloomed on his face. "Oh. Charlotte, I am sorry. I never meant..."

"Yes, you did." The laughing eyes were hard and the normally smiling, sweet face as stiff as those he prepared for the grave. "She didn't turn me funny. She's dead, Father. The dead have no control in this world. Sometimes the soul speaks on, that's all. I'm not 'funny in the head.' You all but admitted I'm as clever as most of the men in your class at school. It's not funny for a woman to want to continue the family business she's grown up around."

She took the small lamp from the table and carried it carefully up the backstairs to the drafty upstairs rooms. Her hand cradled the tall, smoke-stained lamp chimney from the sudden gusts of air as she swished up the passage.

Mr. Harkness hurried up after her, leaving the lamps burning below. "It's not funny. No, it isn't, you're quite right. But there's no future in it."

"Almost one hundred years, Father! Don't tell me we couldn't go one hundred more. You're already far more advanced than any other undertaker in London, save maybe the ones in Kensington and Mayfair, but they have the means to—"

"There you go. Proving you could handle this business." Harkness didn't sound proud, he sounded aggrieved.

Charlotte gave her father a startled, half-hopeful look. He'd never said those words before. "I could?"

"You could. You could do it all, even the things not fit for a woman to do. I have no doubt you could embalm the most foul of corpses while chatting cheerily about what to serve at the funeral luncheon. Perhaps you'd expand our services to offer ready-made hampers for the mourners."

"Oh. That's a thought, Father."

"No! Charlotte, it's not a thought at all. It would be different if you were born a boy. But you weren't and therefore hard truths must be spoken. Let's say that you take over the business. Who will come to you? Which clients?"

"Progressive-minded ones. Women like Mrs. Bailey, possibly. They'll respect a woman's efforts." Or would they doubt a woman's skill?

"Who will help you nail the coffin wood together, do the fittings and the carrying? You can't drive a coach."

"I could learn those things. I could hire help."

"Which men would work for a woman? Where would your profits go?" he demanded.

"I'm certain that someone in the whole of Stepney, or even farther afield, somewhere in Whitechapel, Limehouse, or Bromley, there are two honest men who could heft a wooden box."

Mr. Harkness looked heavenward. "I was too easy on you. I let you read as much as you liked, whatever you could get your hands on, including The Undertaker's Gazette, including The Modern Embalmer's Guide. I've been a blind fool."

"Father, don't be so hard on yourself."

He turned his gaze to her. "You've answered every challenge I've set you. What happens when you wish to retire?"

Silence.

"You'll sell it to one of those honest men? You'll toss away all those generations of the family business? Because you won't have a child of your own like this, Charlotte. You won't find a husband. You won't wed. No one sees you."

"I see people all the time."

"Ah, yes. The vicars and coach drivers, the men in market stalls, the butcher, the grocer, and an occasional widower."

"I'm sorry the annual Undertakers' Ball hasn't seen fit to incorporate a coming-out party for the unfortunate daughters of the dead-mongers." Her tone was biting and bitter. Unsuitable behavior for a woman, I'm sure, to show so much spirit.

"Yes, there's little for you here," her father said slowly, deliberately. "The summer in London is a place of ills and infestations."

Charlotte stepped back, caught off guard by this sudden change of topic. "I suppose it is. Bodies must be buried or embalmed awfully quickly. Perhaps we could look into having the icehouse further insulated?"

"A good thought. Yes, I'll do that. I think that your Aunt Kate would love you to pay her a visit. The air is so bracing up there. It would do you good."

"I see. It will get me away from home? You?"

"Oh no! No, I want you here. Dearest, don't you know how sad and lonely I would have been? I've been selfish long enough, hiding you down here in the shadows and shrouds. You deserve a holiday. Maybe you'll love it."

Maybe I'll magically fall in love with a farmer who wants a wife to help spread manure and birth calves. "Summer is such a busy season."

"All our seasons are busy."

"Death doesn't take holidays. Will you go with me?" Charlotte turned the wick up on the lamp. Her room was small and narrow, simple. She was hardly ever in it. It was a comforting place, dark brown curtains, a red blanket, an old daguerreotype of her mother, and a sketch of Auntie Molly, and books. Books on shelves and stacks of books next to the pile of knitting on her rocking chair. Right now, there was no comfort. Her father, her dearest friend, wanted her to leave. His reasons didn't matter.

"Someone has to mind this place." He laughed weakly. "But a few months away won't matter much. We'll be together again before you know it. Unless, of course, you find you love it up there. Those boys of Kate's, they'll be such good company. Her letters are always full of their tricks, the scamps. Oh, and the Women's Institute and the Parish Ladies Auxiliary... I'm sure they have fun doing"—he groped for words— "all sorts of things!"

"I'm sure they do." Her voice was sad as she sank into the chair beside her bed. She'd never been one to faint or be overcome by the vapors, to fan herself and weakly demand smelling salts. Right now, the weight of her father's forced cheer and the sad smile was smothering her. For the first time ever, she wished her father would simply leave her alone. She wished she had a proper friend to talk to, not just him. He was so clearly against everything she had to say about this, no matter what it was.

"You might find a nice young farmer," he hinted.

"I might find a nice young undertaker here. One interested in joining the family business." The words sprang out of her mouth without thought. She'd met a wide variety of the men in her father's trade, but she hadn't found a single one engaging or attractive. They didn't speak to her like a person, more like a standard reminder of exercising their manners. A dignified and mournful sounding, "Good evening, Miss Harkness," or "Is your father in, Miss Harkness?" had been the extent of their interactions.

Mr. Harkness had been lovingly tracing the frame around his late wife's likeness. Now he lifted his head in surprise. "Yes. Yes, I suppose that could happen."

"Some of these mortuary families are quite large, aren't they?"

"Mr. Parson of Parson and Parson has six children, four of them boys. I believe a few of them are eligible."

"Well..." Charlotte stared at her tightly clasped hands as they rested in her lap. "In some cases, in some of those larger families, perhaps one of the sons would rather strike out on his own, be the head of the business, an opportunity that wouldn't afford itself to all of the sons at once."

"True. Gideon and Danvers, now Mr. Danvers has a son about your age. Peter? You've met Peter?"

"I'm sure I have." She wasn't sure at all. Her heart was pressing into her ribs far harder than her corset stays. I don't love these men. I certainly don't love Peter Danvers, whoever he is! But I love it here. I love the work, I love my father... Many a princess marries for political unions, not for love. I suppose I shall be Queen of the Funeral Directors, forging an alliance between two noble houses. Harkness and Danvers sounds acceptable. Not as good as Harkness and Sons. Or Harkness and Daughter, for that matter.

This is madness, not hearing the soul's echo. To marry a man you don't know if you can stand, simply to stay with the father who by every right should keep you in his home all of your days, if you don't wish to leave his side.

"Have I been a good daughter?" Charlotte asked suddenly, her voice hoarse.

Her father carefully moved her books and knitting, sitting on the footstool as his knees creaked in protest. "The very best of all daughters. Or sons. The very best." He kissed her hand, white at the knuckles, even in the dim light. "No man could ask for better. That's why I only want the very best for you. I want you to be loved and cherished. Healthy and whole. Not alone."

"You're not that old, Father," Charlotte murmured thoughtfully. "You needn't be alone. You're only forty-eight. Many a man has a son later in life. Why, King Henry VIII was only a few years younger than you. Perhaps Harkness and Sons could still—"

"Now, hush. It is unseemly that a girl should give her father such advice." He drew back, flustered. "Furthermore, in my heart and my mind, there is none who can compare to your mother. I want no other."

"A love match," Charlotte murmured, nodding.

His spine stiffened. "Yes. A love match. Ah, your mother was strong, just like you. She had your blue-eyed glare that could make a king cower." He laughed, a short morose bark. "She would give it to me now if she could hear this conversation."

Charlotte imagined she would. What would her mother say if she knew her only daughter, her dumpling, her dear little sparrow, was calmly considering making a match for the sake of saving the family business? Unlike her father, who could but wonder, Charlotte might soon find out.

"I'd like you to find a love match, Charlotte. Your mother would have wanted that as well."

"She wants me to be happy."

"Wants. Not wanted." Reginald's eyes closed briefly. "Yes."

"Being here makes me happy." Charlotte rose, helping her father rise as well, smothering a smile as his back clicked and groaned in perfect unison with his knees. "Now, the next time you see Peter Danvers, you must ask him to tea."

"Are you sure?"

"It needn't be him." Her shoulders rose and fell in resignation. "Feel free to ask someone else instead."

"Dear? This idea of happiness, it is tied to love, at least in some small part. An unhappy marriage..." He trailed off ominously.

"Now then, Father, how can you know it wouldn't be perfect bliss? I've barely met him. It's up to the gentleman to inquire after a lady's interest. He might not take to me."

Mr. Harkness clucked his tongue. "Any man with eyes would take to you, and that is partly the trouble. Any man might wish for your hand. If you take the first offer, any offer, it could end badly."

"There's no pleasing you!" Charlotte laughed and kissed his cheek. "You're going gray with worry that I'll be an old maid, meanwhile you're utterly panicked in case Peter Danvers proposes on sight. What do you want, Father?" she demanded in playful exasperation.

"What do I want? Honestly? A cold mutton sandwich."

With a sigh, she led him back to the kitchen. "I'll finish the wreath for Ned Bailey while you finish a sandwich and what's left of that apple tart."

About the Author

Bestselling author M. Culler can't stick to just one genre. She writes fantasy, mystery, and all flavors of romance. M. Culler lives in historic Chester County, Pennsylvania, where potentially haunted battlegrounds and 17th century buildings serve as never-ending inspiration. M. Culler lives for her family, her community, her students, baking, and Brit Coms. Soli Deo Gloria.

Website and Newsletter[1]
Facebook [2]
Twitter[3]
Amazon[4]
Bookbub [5]
Instagram[6]
Reader's Group: Book Dragons[7]
Historical Heat Historical Romance Group[8]

---

1. https://ghostsintheink.wixsite.com/mculler

2. https://www.facebook.com/MCullerGhostsintheink

3. https://twitter.com/MCullerauthor

4. https://www.amazon.com/M.-Culler/e/B07MZ7KP6S%3Fref=dbs_a_mng_rwt_scns_share

5. https://www.bookbub.com/profile/m-culler

6. https://www.instagram.com/mcullerauthor/

7. https://www.facebook.com/groups/3369871793294694

8. https://www.facebook.com/groups/1704530916569869

Contemporary Romance
Searching Hearts II: Finding Home[9]
Searching Hearts I: Search and Rescue[10]
The Second Santa Solution[11]
Seventh Floor Surprises[12]
Historical Romance/Mystery
The Undertaker's Daughter -Releasing on January 23, 2023
Belling the Tiger(ess) – Coming soon from The Wild Rose
Press
The Earl's Christmas Contest- Coming Soon!
Fantasy
The Mer Parts I-VI[13]
The Mer Parts VII-XII [14]
Jack the Ripper: Demon Hunter[15]

9. http://books2read.com/u/38doWw

10. https://books2read.com/u/mlANJM

11. https://books2read.com/u/mdd8JE

12. http://books2read.com/u/4jgvjY

13. https://books2read.com/u/mgjpJx

14. https://books2read.com/u/4jPXJv

15. https://www.amazon.com/kindle-vella/story/B0B6JGFPT8

www.ingramcontent.com/pod-product-compliance
Lightning Source LLC
LaVergne TN
LVHW040218070725
815500LV00021B/154